HEART LONGING AND THE TREASURE KEYS

An Allegory of the
Treasure of the Kingdom

Julianna Joy Klassen

WESTBOW
PRESS®
A DIVISION OF THOMAS NELSON
& ZONDERVAN

Copyright © 2015 Julianna Joy Klassen.

Artwork by Julie Klassen,
Photographer Elora Rahn

All rights reserved. No part of this book may be used or reproduced by any means, graphic, electronic, or mechanical, including photocopying, recording, taping or by any information storage retrieval system without the written permission of the author except in the case of brief quotations embodied in critical articles and reviews.

WestBow Press books may be ordered through booksellers or by contacting:

WestBow Press
A Division of Thomas Nelson & Zondervan
1663 Liberty Drive
Bloomington, IN 47403
www.westbowpress.com
1 (866) 928-1240

Because of the dynamic nature of the Internet, any web addresses or links contained in this book may have changed since publication and may no longer be valid. The views expressed in this work are solely those of the author and do not necessarily reflect the views of the publisher, and the publisher hereby disclaims any responsibility for them.

Any people depicted in stock imagery provided by Thinkstock are models, and such images are being used for illustrative purposes only. Certain stock imagery © Thinkstock.

ISBN: 978-1-5127-1107-3 (sc)

Library of Congress Control Number: 2015914372

Print information available on the last page.

WestBow Press rev. date: 09/04/2015

Contents

1. "The Treasure Map" 1
2. "Treasure of Egypt" 13
3. "Caught in a Web" 34
4. "The King's Memory Book" 48
5. "A Voice Not Seen" 59
6. "The Plot" 70
7. "A Picnic and a Prisoner' 90
8. "Rescued" 104
9. "Mother Robin's Lesson" 121
10. "A Prized Possession" 133
11. "A Visit to World City" 147
12. "A Secret Bouquet" 157
13. "Eternal Palace" 168

Glossary 179
For You to Think About 181

This book is the sequel to
"Adventures of Heart Longing"
an allegory of the fruit of the Spirit
Galatians 5:22,23

Do not lay up for yourselves treasure on earth,
where moth and rust destroy
and
where thieves break in and steal;
but lay up for yourselves treasure in heaven,
where neither moth nor rust destroys
and
where thieves do not break in and steal,
For where your treasure is, there your heart will be also.

Matthew 6:19,20 NKJV

The Treasure Map as pictured on the back cover can be printed up to poster size – find the high resolution image at www.klassenheartbooks.blogspot.ca

CHAPTER 1

"The Treasure Map"

Heart Longing sat up in bed with a start! What had awakened her? A dream? A sudden sound? She listened ... but all was still. It was too early for anyone to be up, except for a lone bird chirping his unique melody before the lifting darkness of night illuminated the day.

Something had awakened her. But what?

Slowly, she remembered a dream, but pieces were missing. She remembered that something exciting had happened - or was going to happen - but as hard as she concentrated, the rest of the dream's details had faded out of the reach of her conscious mind.

With a sigh she slipped back down under the covers, nestled her head into her pillow and closed her eyes. If she went back to sleep, perhaps she could retrieve her dream. Though she lay for some time, sleep did not come; she was just too wide awake.

She sat up, swung her legs over the side of her bed and stood up. Walking to the window, she moved the blue ruffled curtains to the side, and looked out to see that the sun was just beginning to come up, its pink strokes across the eastern sky announcing the promise of a beautiful spring day.

Unable to shake the feeling that something exciting was beckoning her, hinting of an adventure, she threw on her favourite shorts with the matching blue top and slipped quietly out the front door. Not knowing what else to do, she flopped down into one of the two white wicker chairs on the front porch. She took a deep breath of the fresh morning air that was scented by the grasses and flowers, drunk with the night's dew. Though she looked around carefully, she saw nothing amiss or different in Eternal City; nothing that seemed to give any cause for her sense of expectancy.

It wasn't long before the rest of the family was stirring, and soon Heart's mother called for her to come in for breakfast. Breakfast at the Longing-Fulfilled home that morning was routine; the conversation centered on the plans for the day. Though Heart searched each face around the table, no one else seemed to be expecting anything out of the ordinary to happen.

Heart waited impatiently most of the day, not sure what she was waiting for, but nothing happened. Finally, by late afternoon she was almost ready to concede that her dream was just a dream that meant nothing. Struggling with her sense of disappointment, she left the house and it seemed her feet had a mind of their own, taking her down the path leading to Promise Mountain. She walked with her head down, trying to convince herself to put aside that lingering feeling the dream had left her with.

A soft rustling sound broke into her thoughts, and she looked up to see the leaves of the poplar trees that lined the path, fluttering in the sudden breeze. The wind flipped the leaves up to show their white underside and then, dropped them down again. At first Heart thought it was just her mind playing tricks on her, but when she stopped to listen more carefully she was sure the leaves were teasing her. Every time they moved in the breeze, they whispered ... "we have a secret ... we have a secret ...." Could it be true after all then? WAS something going on in Eternal City? In the grassy field stretching out on the other side of the path, all the daisies and dandelions seemed to eagerly nod their little heads in agreement every time a gust of wind blew across their faces.

Movement caught the corner of Heart's eye. She turned to see two boys coming across the field and heading in her direction. Distance blurred their words, preventing Heart from discerning what they were saying, but there was no mistaking the excitement in their voices. Heart's pulse quickened as she watched the boys approach, fully intending to question them on what they were so excited about. Then, suddenly, they broke into a run, rushing past Heart and completely ignoring her attempts to stop them. *Why in the world were they in such a hurry?* Heart wondered.

She broke into a run to follow them, thinking that maybe she could overtake them, but they soon outdistanced her and she was forced to give up. Resting her hands on her knees until she could catch her breath, she was startled when someone loudly called her name.

Looking back down the way she had come, she saw Sally Self-Less and Lily Truthful running down an embankment toward her. With a big grin, Heart waved and hurried to meet them.

"Hi!" she greeted them, and gave them a quick hug, then asked the question burning in her mind, "Do you know what is going on? Why is everyone so excited?"

"Don't you KNOW?" exclaimed Lily and Sally in one breath of disbelief. "Where have you been? Come on! We'll fill you in as we go!"

Sally grabbed Heart's hand to hurry her along, as they ran sure footed down the well-worn path.

"But where are we going!?" asked Heart impatiently, trying not to step on Lily's heels.

"To Promise Mountain," explained Lily. "We spoke to Word this morning, and asked him what the excitement was all about."

"And you'll never guess what he told us," Sally interrupted. "It's the most exciting thing!"

"Isn't it though!" agreed Lily enthusiastically. The girls had slowed to a brisk walk, but now Lily quickened her pace once more, asking anxiously, "You don't think we'll be late, do you, Sally?"

Heart was ready to burst with frustrated curiosity!

"Late for WHAT? What DID Word say? Will you PLEASE tell me!" she pleaded, her lungs gasping for air.

Sally and Lily burst out in excited laughter. "TREASURE!!" they shouted in unison. "There is treasure hidden in Eternal City!"

"Treasure?" echoed Heart, trying to wrap her mind around it. Questions exploded in her mind. "What kind of treasure? Where is it? Why is it hidden? How do we find it?"

Sally and Lily laughed at Heart's impatient string of questions. "That's what we are hurrying to find out. Word has said he'll meet us at Promise Mountain, and he's going to tell us all about it. OH! Come on! Let's not waste time talking!"

The three girls broke into a run, Lily dashing ahead with Heart and Sally close behind. They did not stop until the path ended at the foot of Promise Mountain. The mountain rose high and majestic. The white clouds shrouding the peak were beginning to glow with evening pink. The sun rays reflecting on little pools of water made them look like scattered jewels across the mountain slope. The early spring flowers bloomed in colourful bouquets, tucked among evergreen shrubs and mountain heather. It was a breathtaking sight, but no one seemed to be taking notice of it.

A crowd had already gathered, and everyone was talking at once. Their excited voices rose and fell, blending together in a sound like that of rushing water tumbling over rocks and pebbles.

The three girls eagerly pressed into the crowd, not wanting to miss anything.

"Is Word here yet?" Sally asked the older man standing beside her.

The man turned to Sally, the tense lines in his face almost relaxing into a shadow of a smile as he looked down at her, then he replied, "No, he has not come yet. We are all waiting for him."

Heart looked around at the people in the crowd. She recognized several faces - some friends, some not. Gwen Greedy was there with Gail Quarrelsome. Pride was there, surrounded by his friends. Honey Sweet was talking to a girl Heart did not know. Star Light stood some distance in front of Heart; she turned just then and catching sight of Heart, waved eagerly. To Heart's surprise her brother Trouble-Free was there as well. Mrs. Abider and Mrs. Servant were standing in a group talking to Heart's parents. Even Mrs. Idle Hand was there. It looked as though just about everyone was gathered there, waiting.

The word "treasure" was on every tongue and Heart listened, as the word bounced from mouth to mouth and back again, like an endless echo. Studying the faces around her, she noted that some wore obvious expressions of eagerness, some were clouded with anxiety, some simply curious and some she could not read - but one thing was evident, everyone shared the same impatient expectancy she felt.

Oh Word, please hurry, Heart thought as loudly as she could. *I can't bear the suspense much longer.*

Hearing an audible wave of excitement sweep over the crowd, Heart stretched up on her toes to try to look over or around the people in front of her. She saw that Word was indeed approaching them.

The rhythmic sound of his horse's hoof beats was muffled by the rustle of the crowd, but nothing could dim the light that always radiated from Word and yet shone upon him. His armour glinted and flashed swords of light that made those watching shade their eyes. The rich copper colour of his hair was deepened by the glorious light, and his face was so beautifully wise and altogether lovely that as he came near and pulled up his horse, an awe-filled hush fell over the crowd.

How beautiful he is, thought Heart. *When I see him and listen to his messages, I always feel so close to the King. I guess it's because Word always comes from being with King Vine and brings his Presence with him.*

Word dismounted and held up his hand to indicate he was about to speak.

The crowd, now hushed, breathed as one. Each pair of eyes fastened on Word, and every ear strained to hear Word's message. Everyone's thoughts were focused on the promise that there was treasure they could gain for themselves. Treasure that would change their lives.

Finally, Word began to speak. "I know what is uppermost in all of your minds - finding treasure. And I have come to tell you that, yes, the rumours you have heard are true. There is indeed treasure hidden in Eternal City – beautiful, priceless treasure!"

A roar erupted, expressing the excited enthusiasm of the crowd. Word waited until everyone's attention was once more riveted on him, and then he continued. "Anyone desiring to search for this treasure may have one of my treasure maps." As he spoke, Word held up the bundle of maps he had brought with him.

Instantly, the crowd surged forward, everyone reaching, pushing to be among the first to receive a map. They were ready to begin their search for hidden treasure immediately, hoping to gain the advantage of a head start.

Heart watched, somewhat dismayed at the people's frenzied impatience to get their hands on one of Word's maps. What was it she read in so many of the faces ... was it the same longing she felt deep within to know and follow the King? Or was it greed focused on satisfying selfish desires?

Heart's thoughts took her back to when she and her family had first come to meet King Vine, and he had renamed the Longing family, Longing-Fulfilled. It was true. That deep restless longing that nothing could satisfy had been fulfilled and quieted with peace when she met King Vine at the cross. But then, a new longing had been birthed within her - a sweeter, more intense longing. Heart smiled gently to herself. It seemed the more she came to know King Vine, the more she longed to know him better.

Heart stood at the edge of the crowd and waited until it had thinned, and most of the people had rushed off with their coveted maps clutched in their hands.

Finally, Heart approached Word. "May I have a map too, please, Word?" she requested. "The treasure sounds wonderful, but exactly what am I to look for?"

Word handed Heart a map, and began to climb the path up Promise Mountain without answering her question. Heart automatically fell into step beside him.

It really was a beautiful mountain. Every inch was in fact a garden most carefully planned and cared for. Every tree, every flower, every rock, each blade of grass added to the completeness and perfection of the garden. Even the stones, carefully laid to provide a walkway for travellers, created a pattern pleasing to the eye. Everything had a place, a purpose, fitting into the detailed design of its creator. The colours blended their hues in such glory that anyone studying the mountain was compelled to gasp in pure delight and wonder.

On any other day, Heart would have drunk eagerly of the beauty around her, but today her full attention was focused on what Word was saying.

"King Vine desires you to gather treasure for yourself," Word explained. "He has hidden it hoping that you will find it. Some of the treasure you find will give you much pleasure and be useful in the Kingdom now, but all of it King Vine will store for you to enjoy throughout all eternity."

Word suddenly became very serious. "You must beware, dear Heart, because there are two kinds of treasure. One kind may glitter and shine, but in a short time it will be destroyed by rust and decay, or it will be stolen by thieves. Stay far away from this kind of treasure, Heart, for it will bring you only trouble and grief. This is what is called 'treasure of Egypt'. It is a fool's treasure. The treasure the King has hidden is treasure that nothing can destroy, and no-one can steal. It is kept safe with him until the day that you will go to be with him forever in his Palace. His treasure is Eternal treasure."

Heart listened, enraptured.

Then, looking up at Word, her eyes wide with awe at the new thought, she asked, "Live with King Vine in His Palace? I have never seen His Palace. Where is it?"

She had been listening so intently to Word, that she had not realized how high they had climbed on Promise Mountain. Never before had she reached this height.

Now, stopping to look at the view, she caught her breath in wonder. It was magnificent beyond description. Word looked into her upturned face and answered softly, "It lies before us; you are gazing at it!"

In the distance, as though suspended in space, was a far more splendid, glorious Palace than Heart could ever have imagined. She continued to stare wide-eyed and speechless, unable to find any words to describe its majesty and glory.

The air surrounding the Palace was filled with countless tiny flecks of gold dust that glittered and shone in the glory light radiating from the Palace. The precious stones with which the Palace was built caught, and reflected, and magnified the brilliant radiance so that it all but blinded Heart's eyes.

Finally, Heart released her breath in one long swoosh. "Oh, please, Word, could we go closer?" she pleaded, somehow knowing that she could not, yet an overwhelming flood of emotions drew her toward the Palace.

"I am sorry," answered Word, "But it is not yet possible for you to go any closer."

It was then that Heart noticed a high wall between her and the shining diamond sea surrounding the Palace. In the wall was a huge black door that was securely closed. On this door were written the letters that spelled "DEATH".

Heart Longing and the Treasure Keys

"But why?" cried Heart, filled with dismay. "Why does such a beautiful place have such an awful looking door? Why must it keep me out? Why can I not go in?"

"Heart," explained Word in a gentle voice, "King Vine longs more than you could know for the day when you will enter his Palace. That door named 'DEATH' is the only way you can enter the Palace, and it is not yet your time. There are things that the King has planned for you to do and experience. You must prepare yourself to spend eternity with him. When you come, he desires that you come with much treasure awaiting you so that you can share in his glory with great joy!"

It all sounded so gloriously wonderful that Heart did not want to wait. She wanted to go NOW! Everything within her reached for, and longed to be on the other side of that wall – yet – at the same time, there was also within her a strong fear of going through that black door. Word seemed to understand the thoughts and emotions tumbling in Heart's mind.

"Do not fear, Heart," he comforted, "King Vine's ways are just and true. He has planned all things well, and even though you cannot yet go to him in his Palace, his Presence is with you. His eyes are ever upon you; he cares for you and he loves you always."

"I know, and his promises are wonderful," answered Heart softly, feeling the Presence encircle her like a loving embrace. "I know King Vine knows best in all things. I trust him and I believe all he says."

Heart had almost forgotten the excitement of the day, but now she held up the treasure map in her hand.

"I will search for treasure, Word, and I will find it so that I will have much treasure waiting for me when I go to King Vine in his Palace. I will follow your map very carefully," Heart promised.

With one long last lingering look at Eternal Palace glowing in the warm colours of the setting sun, Heart turned and ran all the way down the mountain, eager for tomorrow to come so she and her friends could together begin to search for the hidden treasure!

CHAPTER 2

"Treasure of Egypt"

An older man, dressed in jogging clothes suitable for an early morning run, paused at a white gate to lean over it and call out a cheery morning greeting.

"Hello! What have you got there that's so interesting this lovely morning?" he asked.

Receiving no response, he called again, a little louder, "Hello! Good Morning!"

His eyes twinkled good-naturedly as he stood for a time, watching three girls sitting on a bench some distance from the gate. They were bent over something spread out on their lap and they were so intently focused on it, that the jogger could see they took no notice of anything else around them.

After several moments he continued on his morning jog, smiling to himself and wondering what could be so interesting to three girls that early in the morning. Had he not been new to Eternal City, he might have guessed that it was the treasure map that had the three friends up so early that morning.

Heart, Sally Self-Less and Lily Truthful were indeed so deeply engrossed in studying their maps, that they had not heard anyone shouting a greeting to them.

"Ohhhh!" Sally suddenly exploded, discouragement evident in her voice. She threw her hands in the air, sending the map flying to the ground. "This map is so hard to understand, I don't think we'll EVER find any treasure."

"We can't give up so easily, "encouraged Heart, as she quickly grabbed the map before the wind could blow it across the yard. "Treasure maps are never easy to understand. If they were too obvious, then there would be no point in hiding the treasure. King Vine does not want his enemies to find the treasure, only those who truly seek to please him will find it."

Lily and Sally stared at Heart with a new respect, then thoughtfully agreed. "That is true," said Lily. "We cannot give up until we find it. Word would not have given us a map that is impossible to understand. Not easy, but not impossible either. Come on, Sally, help us try again!"

"All right," agreed Sally with a sigh, and bent her head once more over the puzzling map.

There was another concentrated silence for several minutes, then Lily suddenly let out a shout that made both Sally and Heart jump!

"I think I've got it!" Lily cried.

"What? You do? Tell us!" begged Heart and Sally in eager unison.

"Look, it's really quite easy." Lily's words tumbled over each other in breathless confidence. "The treasure hunt starts here." She pointed to the cross at the bottom corner of the map, beside which was a key indicating hidden treasure. "To find eternal treasure we must start at the cross. Remember the day we met the King there?"

All three girls remembered well their journey to the cross. Heart thought back to the day she had come to Eternal City and had followed Humble's directions. She had met King Vine at the cross, seen his love, received his cleansing forgiveness and had become a citizen of Eternal City. Then some time later she had led Sally Selfish and Lily Liar to the cross, where they too had met the King, experienced his loving forgiveness, and had entered his Kingdom. It was then he had given them their new names – Sally Selfish became Sally Self-Less and Lily Liar became Lily Truthful. Since then, Heart, Sally, and Lily had become the best of friends.

Sally brought them back to the present. "I get it!" she exclaimed. "See the treasure sign here at the cross? It means that there we will find the first treasure."

"Hey, I think you are right!" agreed Heart. "Now why didn't I see that right away?"

A puzzled frown creased Sally's forehead. "Okay, but what do we do now? Do we get shovels and start digging near the cross?"

"Hmm...." The girls' excitement was suddenly squelched, as they realized that they still had no idea how to go about getting the treasure.

Then Lily said slowly, "Shovels and digging doesn't somehow sound quite right ... but it must have something to do with the key that is shown there. What do you think the key would unlock?"

"I know what we need to do. We need to go find Word and ask him. He will tell us!" declared Sally, realizing she had no answer to Lily's question.

"Good idea," agreed Heart.

Heart carefully folded up her map, and put it in her pocket. She then joined her friends to look for Word. As they walked along, arm in arm, they could not ignore the fact that it was a lovely day; the sun shone its warm beams down from a cloudless sky. A perfect day for a treasure hunt, if only they knew how to go about it!

As usual, Word was not hard to find. They had not gone far when they found him. He and his horse were resting beneath the Wisdom Tree whose branches reached out over the Stream of Refreshing. The three friends sat down on the soft grass beside Word. Heart pulled out her map, smoothing it open in front of her. Looking up to catch Word's attention, she pointed to the sign of treasure beside the cross.

Heart Longing and the Treasure Keys

"See, Word," Heart explained, "we've figured out that we must start searching for treasure at the cross. But we don't understand how we are to find this treasure. What does it look like? We didn't really think that digging would be the right thing to do, and what does the key mean, where do we find it, and what does it unlock?"

Word smiled down at the three eager faces turned up to hear his instruction. Heart, gazing into Word's face, for a moment forgot her question. When Word smiled, the light around him took on an added glow, and Heart smiled back, not realizing that as she did, her own smile reflected the glow from Word's face.

"No," chuckled Word, in response to Heart's question. "No, digging is not the way to find treasure. But you are right in that the first treasure is found at the cross. When you came to the cross, putting your trust in King Vine, you were given his promise of Eternal Life and the key to Eternal City. Your Eternal Life treasure was put into your treasure chest in the Eternal Palace, where no one can ever steal it from you." Word reached into his pocket, and handed something to each of the girls. "Here are the keys that will unlock the treasure of eternal life. I've been keeping one for each of you."

In awe, each of the girls admired her beautiful key that hung from a crimson cord twisted with golden threads. They were silent, trying to absorb what Word had told them.

Heart spoke first. "We have a treasure chest in Eternal Palace?" she asked in astonishment.

"Yes, indeed!" assured Word.

Three pairs of eyes were wide with wonder. "Seriously? And we each have the Treasure of Eternal Life in our treasure chests? Are our names on these chests? And these keys really unlock our treasure?" It was hard to believe. They stared at their keys, then at Word, trying to understand the wonderful truth of what Word was telling them.

"Yes, it is true!" repeated Word with a smile. "Your names are written on your treasure chests, and each of you has the treasure of Eternal Life in your chest. The King desires all his citizens to fill their chest to overflowing with beautiful treasure. You will experience much joy brought by the treasure - both now in the finding of it, and also when the time comes for you to go to Eternal Palace, to enjoy your treasure forever!"

The girls waved and shouted their thank-yous as they watched Word ride off toward Promise Mountain. When he was out of sight, Sally turned to her friends and said, "Can you believe it? I've never heard anything so exciting. Not only do we have our first treasure, but we even have a treasure chest in Eternal Palace to keep it in."

Lily and Heart readily agreed; it was truly wonderful! Again and again, they admired their keys and imagined how beautiful their treasure must be.

Hand in hand, they had begun to walk away from the Wisdom Tree, following the banks of the Stream of Refreshing as it wound down the hillside. They were so busy in their thoughts and conversation that they did not notice when they first turned away from the stream and began heading toward a barren field.

Heart Longing and the Treasure Keys

Neither did they notice when the tone of their conversation began to change. At first, their conversation had centered on the joy of finding treasure and the fact that the King was keeping it for them in Eternal Palace. But then their thoughts began to wander, and they wondered if they were the only ones to have discovered treasure. Feeling that they had perhaps accomplished what others had not, soon gave room for covetous thoughts to slip into their minds. They began to entertain these thoughts and feed them. Their conversation ceased, and they walked in silence, each thinking about ways that she could keep all this wonderful treasure for herself. They even began to wonder if maybe it would be better if they each did their own searching, rather than share any clues they found that would lead to treasure – and then have to share the treasure as well. They did not notice that they had lingered under Self-Peak Falls and then passed through Selfish Park.

"What was that?" Heart broke the silence, suddenly stopping to tilt her head, listening intently.

The other girls stopped too. "I don't hear anything," said Lily.

"Wait!" cried Lily. "I hear it too. What is it?"

"Perhaps if we walk toward the sound, we'll be able to find out," suggested Lily.

"Yes," agreed Heart, then pointed toward a hedge of bramble bushes. "It is definitely coming from over there."

As they cautiously approached the bramble hedge, the sound of shouting and the noise of excited voices was unmistakeable.

"What is going on?" asked Heart, wondering if there was any cause for alarm.

"I don't know ... let's go see," prompted Lily.

They pushed aside the bramble bushes that scratched their hands, and arms, and caught at their clothing. When they finally broke through the last bush, they came upon an incredible sight.

There, spread out before them was a city; not an ordinary city, but a city that glittered and gleamed with flashing coloured lights. The boldly coloured stones, set into the walls of the buildings, caught and threw back the rays of colour hitting them with such intensity, they had to squint their eyes. Garishly painted signs beckoned everywhere, promising pleasure and treasure at every turn. The streets were filled with people laughing and dancing, dressed in gaily coloured clothing. The voices of men, shouting to sell their wares, cut through the loud music that filled the air. It was as though the whole city had exploded into festivity, and everything moved and throbbed with its hypnotic beat.

The girls stared with open mouths, feeling themselves repelled, yet, irresistibly drawn into the frenzied merry making.

Sally looked at Heart and Lily and asked, "What do you think, should we go down and join in the fun?"

A hesitancy shadowed Heart's mind, and she answered slowly. "I don't know." She wanted to go but ... was that a warning whispering in her mind to turn back?

"Would it hurt just to go down and look around?" questioned Sally.

"Well, no, I guess not," Heart agreed reluctantly, trying to find words to describe the uneasy feeling inside of her. Yet, she could not deny that she too was curious to take a closer look.

So the three girls linked arms and went down to the city. They entered it, and walked up the broad street that cut through the middle of the city. It was almost impossible not to react to the wild excitement that throbbed around them.

Heart suddenly stopped and grabbed Lily's arm. "Look," she pointed, "there's Pride and Gwen Greedy."

Pride and Gwen Greedy noticed the girls just at that same moment, and they immediately crossed the busy street to join them.

"Hi!" greeted Pride easily, as though he was not at all surprised to see them. "If you're looking for treasure, you've come to the right place. There is treasure galore! Look at all we've found." Pride opened the chest he was carrying under his arm and showed Heart, Lily and Sally the glittering gems and stones inside. The girls gasped in delight and admiration.

"What beautiful treasure!" they exclaimed, not pausing to wonder why Pride carried his treasure chest with him when Word had told them theirs was in Eternal Palace.

"Where did you find it?" asked Heart, eagerly.

"It's everywhere!" laughed Pride. "There for the taking, I can show you!"

"Let them find it for themselves." Gwen Greedy spoke for the first time. "Why should we help them find it?" She scowled at the girls, and walked off, disappearing through the doorway of a nearby building.

"Aw... don't listen to her, there's lots for everyone." Pride spoke in a soothing tone. "Come, there's someone I want you to meet."

Heart and her friends followed Pride as he deftly wound his way in and out of the crowds, up one street and down another, until he stopped in front of a large imposing house. It stood tall, with three stories and big round pillars on either side of the wide front door. It would have been impressive if it had not been painted black with grey pillars and trim.

"This is the home of a friend of mine," he bragged. "His name is Mr. Destroyer, and he is the mayor of this city. Come, I'll introduce you to him."

Pride walked boldly up the long walk, took the steps two at a time and then knocked his fist loudly on the front door.

A large man opened the door. His hair was black, his brows bushy and thick, and his eyes were as black as his hair. He was dressed in a shiny black suit with a heavy brass chain around his neck that drew immediate attention simply by providing such stark contrast to the rest of his apparel.

"Hello!" he welcomed in a booming voice. "Come in, come in, Pride, and bring your friends with you. Your friends are always welcome here." Pride turned, grinning and gestured with his hand for Heart and her friends to come join him. He waited until they stood behind him at the open front door.

Pride was obviously quite at home in Mr. Destroyer's home, judging by how confidently he led the girls into a large room and invited them to choose where they would like to sit down. Mr. Destroyer leaned against the wall, watching with approval. Their feet sank into the gaudy orange carpet that cushioned their feet as they walked over to one of the several huge pillowed black couches in the room. Heart sat down and looked around. Never had she been in a room anything like this. Glaring lamps stood beside grotesque carved statues. Brass figurines sat in each corner. Heart found it hard to draw her gaze away from their strangely hypnotic eyes that seemed to come alive in the glow from the burning incense they held in their laps. The walls were wildly patterned in loud colours. Metallic chains hanging from the ceiling caught the light from the lamps and twisted it into the eerie patterns reflected back onto the ceiling and walls. Though the lamps projected a glaring light, they did not seem to have the power to reach the darkened corners of the room. The whole effect churned Heart's stomach and she thought maybe she would be ill. She looked at Lily and Sally to see if they felt the same and the greenish hue of their faces told her they too were not feeling comfortable.

Just then Mr. Destroyer demanded loudly, "Well, have you found any treasure yet?"

The girls looked at each other, relieved to be able to talk about something that they knew. They eagerly began tell of their eternal treasure, but their words withered uncomfortably on their tongues when Mr. Destroyer's black brows drew down over his black eyes as he stared at them. Narrowing his eyes, he glared at them seeming to be able to read their very thoughts. To the girls' relief, he abruptly turned and walked over to an ornate desk. He pulled open a drawer and took out a fistful of glittering jewels, offering a handful to each girl. They admired them and hesitantly thanked him. Heart clutched her jewels tightly, thinking that perhaps she had been a little hasty in her judgement of Mr. Destroyer. Covertly, she dropped her treasure into her pocket.

Mr. Destroyer rang a bell, and almost immediately a girl appeared, with the most unhappy face Heart had ever seen. He sharply ordered the girl to bring juice and cookies for his guests.

Wait until I go home and tell everyone that I was served treats at the mayor of Egypt's house, thought Heart. The jewels in her pocket and the promise of juice and cookies had almost made her forget that uneasy feeling in the pit of her stomach. She slipped her hand back into her pocket to finger the precious gems, and as if Mr. Destroyer could read her thoughts, his lips curled into a smile. Shyly, Heart smiled back.

While they enjoyed the delicious cookies and juice the girl served them, Heart noticed that the girl never smiled. In fact, she never said a word, while Mr. Destroyer, on the other hand, did his best to make them feel welcome in his city.

"I'm so glad you've come," he flattered. "I want you to be special guests of my city today. You may go anywhere and do whatever you like. Enjoy yourselves and find as much treasure as you can."

Mr. Destroyer laughed and again his eyes fastened on Heart. She never knew if it was something evil she heard in his laugh, or something she saw in his cold eyes that never warmed with his smile - but suddenly, she was sure, very sure, that they must leave immediately. They were in grave danger.

"Let's go," she stage whispered to Sally and Lily.

The girls stood up and without saying good-bye, hurried out of the house. They ignored the insistent shouts of Mr. Destroyer that they stay just a little longer.

Pride followed them outside.

"Why did you leave so suddenly?" he demanded. "There was so much more I wanted Mr. Destroyed to show you!"

"We had to leave. There was something wrong in there," explained Lily. Heart glanced at her thinking, *so Lily did feel it too.*

Sally nodded, agreeing that she as well was very relieved to leave Mr. Destroyer's home.

Pride quickly changed the subject. "Come then and play some of our city's games; they are such fun!"

Before the girls could reply, someone called out to Pride from one of the doorways across the street. It was Gwen Greedy.

"Hey, Pride," she shouted. "Come on over here and see what we found."

Pride ran over to where Gwen was standing, and they both disappeared into the building, the door swinging shut behind them. The three friends were left abandoned in the street, but they were not sorry to see Pride go.

"What do we do now?" asked Sally.

No one had any suggestions, so they began to walk up the street, gazing with curious amazement at all the attractions, and various enticements around them. Nightfall was coming, but the city flashed on more and more neon lights that forced the darkness into corners and pushed the shadows back behind the buildings.

Heart suddenly gasped, and pointed to a sign bigger and higher than all the rest. It read "CITY OF EGYPT".

"What's the matter, Heart?" asked Sally and Lily, both alarmed to see the colour drain from Heart's face.

"We're in the wrong place," replied Heart, with a sick feeling in the pit of her stomach. "Word warned me yesterday about Egypt and its treasures. He told me to stay far away from it. We have to get out of here, NOW!"

The girls looked around them. "But which way is out?" asked Lily, fearfully. Heart, and Sally too, were filled with dismay. Which way, indeed! All the streets looked the same and there were no exit signs posted anywhere.

"I think it's that way," suggested Sally, putting on a brave face, but not at all sure it really was the right way. Since no one had a better plan, the girls began to walk in the direction Sally had pointed.

They held onto each other and walked as fast as they could, looking neither to the left nor to the right, ignoring the voices calling out to them with enticing promises of pleasure.

It seemed they had walked for hours, when their surroundings began to look strangely familiar.

"Heart, Sally!" The distress in Lily's voice alerted her friends to the fact that something must be terribly wrong. "We're in awful trouble! This is where we were when we started to look for a way out."

"You mean," wailed Sally, "that we have just walked and walked in one big circle?"

They had! After all this time, they were no closer to finding their way out than when they had begun, and now nightfall was upon them. What were they going to do?

"Let's find someone who can help us," suggested Sally in desperation. "Someone must know how to get out of Egypt."

"Of course," Heart and Lily agreed, with relief. Why hadn't they thought of that before? They looked around to find someone that might be trustworthy enough to give them directions.

Not far away, was a little café with an open take-out window. They could see a young man moving inside. The girls approached the window, and Sally cleared her throat to get the man's attention.

"Excuse me?" she said, when the sound of clearing her throat was ignored.

The young man finally turned to look at them and asked, "Well, what do you want to order?" Taken aback by his scowling face and unfriendly manner, Sally hesitated.

"Come on, come on," he snarled. "I haven't got all night!"

The smell of food made the girls realize that they had had nothing to eat since they had those cookies in Mr. Destroyer's house, but Heart said quickly, "We don't want any food. We don't want to buy anything. We just want to ask if you know the way out of Egypt. Could you give us directions, please?"

The man stared, then snorted. "Leave Egypt? Whatever would you want to do that for? Where would you go?" He turned to someone behind him and shouted, "Would you believe it? There are three girls here who want to know how to get out of Egypt!" Both roared with laughter, ignoring the girls still standing at the window.

"Let's go," said Lily finally. "They obviously can't or won't help us."

"What are we going to do?" It was the question in all their minds, but none had an answer. They wished desperately that they had never found this horrible place.

"Look," said Sally suddenly, barely above a whisper. The girls followed the direction of her pointing finger and could just make out the figure of an old man sitting in the shadow of an obviously time-worn building. "Maybe he can help us."

Cautiously, the girls approached the hunched over figure that had not moved since they had noticed him. He seemed unaware of their approach until they were almost beside him.

"Oooooh ...." He finally acknowledged them, straining his eyes in the dim light. "I don't think I know you. Have I seen you before?"

"No, you haven't," answered Heart politely, feeling encouraged that he spoke to them in a civil tone of voice. "We do not belong here. We should never have come. Now we want to get out, but can't find the way. Could you perhaps help us?"

The girls looked at him hopefully, holding their breath.

The man was silent for a long moment, then he sadly said, "Should never have come, shouldn't have come." He repeated these words over and over in a slow chant. "You should not have come." He gazed at the girls for a long time then he asked, "What are your names?"

Heart Longing and the Treasure Keys

"I'm Heart Longing-Fulfilled, this is Sally Self-Less and this is Lily Truthful," Heart answered for all of them.

"What beautiful names you have, what lovely names, they do not belong here."

The old man's voice faded, and he stared absent mindedly into the darkness.

"What is YOUR name?" asked Sally, hoping to recapture his attention.

"My name? My name?" asked the old man slowly, after a long pause. "My name is Mr. Regret." His attention drifted again; he seemed lost in his own thoughts.

"Please, please, Mr. Regret," begged Heart, "do you know how to get out of Egypt?"

"Get out?" the old man repeated, then sat silent, his brow knit in deep thought. Finally, he said, "Yes, I seem to remember that there is a way out. I looked for it a long, long time ago and I found it. But I didn't take it, I should have gone, I should have. Why didn't I go?" he asked sadly.

"If you remember where it is," encouraged Sally hopefully, "we could all go out together. We'll help you."

"Oh ... how kind of you, but it is too late, too late," lamented the old man. "I should have gone a long time ago. Now it is too late. Much too late."

"It's never too late," pleaded Lily. "Oh please try! Try to remember the way."

"I remember," said Mr. Regret so quietly the girls leaned forward to hear him. "I remember the way was hidden, it was narrow, it was almost never used."

"But where was it?" Heart urged gently. "Please try to remember."

"So long ago, so long ago … I haven't thought about it for a long time." He was silent for several moments. The girls almost gave up hope that he would speak again, but then he spoke once more.

"The way was not far from me. I saw it, not far away, but I did not go, I did not go. I should have gone, I should have gone." His voice trailed away and he closed his eyes as if to shut out both by-gone memories and the conversation that reminded him of them.

"Where do we start looking?" asked Heart, realizing that Mr. Regret had told them all he knew.

"Well, he did say it was nearby. He must have meant around here somewhere," answered Lily thoughtfully.

The girls looked back at the bustling, noisy city, then back at the shadows surrounding the old man and his tumble down home.

"If it is a way not much used," noted Sally," it must be around here. This is the only place we've seen that is not busy and full of people and activity."

"You are right," agreed Heart and Lily. "Let's search around here."

Not really sure what they were looking for, the three girls began to cover the area around the old man's house. Though they searched carefully, they found nothing that looked like a path of escape. They saw the discouragement in each other's faces.

Heart Longing and the Treasure Keys

Then Heart had one last idea. "The only place we haven't searched is directly behind Mr. Regret's house."

"But it's so dark there, we can't see anything," protested Lily and Sally. "And if it is directly behind his own house, how could Mr. Regret have forgotten where it was?"

"We have to at least try. There's nowhere else to look. It's our last hope," said Heart, sounding braver than she felt. "We'll hold hands and stay together."

Carefully, the girls shuffled through the tall weeds and grasses toward Mr. Regret's back yard. It was so dark they could hardly see their hands in front of their faces. They stood still, hoping their eyes would adjust to the blackness, and as they waited they noticed something else. They realized that the noise of the city had suddenly grown strangely dim.

Lily began to feel excited. "I think we're close, I think we're going to find it!"

"I do so hope you are right," answered Heart, encouraged by Lily's enthusiasm. Just at that moment, Sally stumbled and fell, pulling Heart and Lily, domino effect, down with her. "Ohhh!" she cried out in pain. "I've hurt my leg!"

Immediately concerned, Heart and Lily knelt at their friend's side. "Are you badly hurt? Can you stand up?"

Sally rubbed her leg, then seemed to forget all about her injury. "LOOK! LOOK!" she cried out with joy, instead of pain.

Heart and Lily wondered at the sudden change in Sally's voice, and they looked down to where Sally was smoothing away the grass. There in the ground was a sign post almost completely hidden by the weeds and underbrush that had grown up around and over it. Now as the girls stared at it, trying to make out what it said, it began to glow with a soft light, almost as though it had an inner lamp of its own.

The girls read the illuminated words in unison, "WAY PROVIDED".

This is it!" they shouted with joy and relief. "We have found it! We've found it!"

"Let's go! Can you run, Sally? Do you need help?" asked Heart anxiously.

"Yes, yes, I'm fine," assured Sally Self-Less, "But what about Mr. Regret? Shouldn't we take him with us?"

"Yes, of course," agreed Heart and Lily quickly. They ran back to where the old man was still sitting, mumbling over and over again, "I should have gone, now it's too late. It's too late."

"No, no, it's not too late," urged the girls. "We've found the way. It's still there. You can come with us. We'll help you."

"It's too late for me," Mr. Regret insisted, almost as though he had not heard them. "I could have gone back then, but I didn't."

The girls pleaded and begged but to no avail. The old man refused to move. Finally, they reluctantly gave up and returned to where they had found the 'WAY PROVIDED' sign post.

As fast as they could, they hurried along the darkened path but the farther they went, the brighter it became, until once again, they saw the Stream of Refreshing reflecting the glow of the full moon.

"Oh, look!" shouted Heart with great relief. "We're out! We're back in Eternal City."

The girls hugged each other, ecstatic to be out of Egypt at last.

Heart felt something pressing in her pocket and remembered the treasure they had gotten in Egypt.

"No!" she cried in dismay. "We have taken the treasure with us. What shall we do with it?" She put her hand in her pocket, but all she pulled out were some rusty crumbs that dirtied her hand as they sifted through her fingers.

Sally's and Lily's treasure had also crumbled with decay. Each looked at the worthless treasure in her hand and Heart remembered what Word had said, "Treasure of Egypt will decay or be stolen."

He was right. How thankful the three friends were to have escaped from that terrible city.

CHAPTER 3

"Caught in a Web"

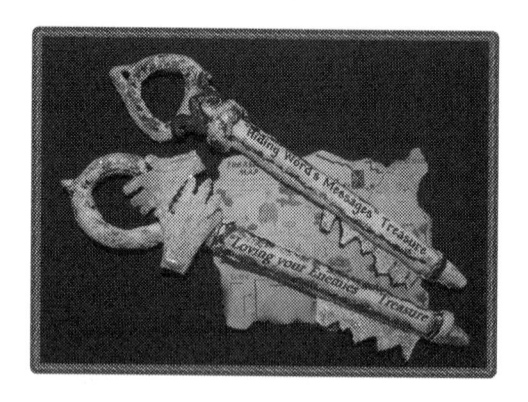

"Lily," greeted Sally Self-Less when Lily answered the knock on her door. "I'm going down to Heart's house. We're going to look for more treasure. Can you come too?"

"Oh, of course, I'd love to come," agreed Lily. "Just a minute, I'll check with Mom."

Lily left Sally at the door and slipped into the kitchen to think for a moment. She had a problem. Just before Sally had knocked at the door, her mother had told her that she needed her help to weed the flower beds in her garden. The Garden

Heart Longing and the Treasure Keys

Society committee was coming around the next day to take photos for the 'Best Garden Contest'. Lily's mom was hoping she could win (back to back) two years in a row. While Lily wanted her mom to win, she really hated weeding; she would so much rather go treasure hunting with her friends. By the time Lily found her mother in the laundry room, folding the clothes fresh out of the dryer, she had formulated a plan. She knew what she would do.

Lily's mother looked up when Lily entered the room. "Do you need something, Lily?" she asked, searching Lily's face.

"Mom," began Lily, uncomfortably aware of her Mother's gaze. "Heart Longing is very ill, and her mother has asked if Sally and I could go over and sit with her. I know you wanted me to help with the garden today, but…. " Lily let her voice trail away, hoping she sounded convincing enough.

"Oh, poor Heart!" responded Lily's mother immediately. "Never mind about the garden, I'll do the best I can and if I win, I win - if not, that's okay too. It's more important that you go cheer up dear little Heart. She's such a nice girl. I do hope she's not seriously ill."

"Thanks, Mom," said Lily, ignoring the guilt that tugged at her. *Oh well,* she thought, trying to excuse herself, *pulling out weeds is not nearly as important as searching for treasure. Mom just wouldn't understand."*

Sally was still waiting at the door. "Can you come?" she asked eagerly, when Lily reappeared.

"Yes," answered Lily," just wait until I get my shoes on."

The two girls walked over to the Longing-Fulfilled home to pick up Heart. Heart's brother, Trouble-Free and his friend were just leaving the house.

"Hi," they greeted Lily and Sally. "We're off treasure hunting. How about you?"

"The same," laughed Sally. "Hope you find lots and lots!"

"Come on in!" called Heart, leaning out the front door. "I'm just finishing my breakfast. Do you want something? Some juice or something?"

"Sure, thanks," chorused Sally and Lily, following Heart into the house. Heart poured two more glasses of orange juice.

Her treasure map was lying on the table, and the three girls sat down to plan their next excursion.

"Where did we go wrong yesterday?" asked Sally. "How come we ended up in Egypt?"

"I think I understand, "explained Heart. "I've been studying the map. We started here." She pointed to the cross. "And that was right. Then if you look closely, we should have gone this way. There's a little arrow here and the directions say, 'HIDE WORD'S MESSAGES IN YOUR HEART'. Word told me to beware of Egypt and its treasure. He told me about how it is fool's treasure and not the real thing, but I forgot. When we started thinking proud, covetous thoughts about finding the treasure all for ourselves, we left the narrow path, wandered through Selfish Park and then, bush wacked through this thick undergrowth to find that back way into Egypt."

"You are right, of course," agreed both Lily and Sally. "A selfish and greedy attitude will always lead us astray and make us forget Word's warning. So what we need to do now is hide Word's messages – listen carefully to what he says and memorize his words. Has anyone spoken to Word this morning?"

No one had, so the girls finished their drinks and set out to find him. The morning had that freshness about it that comes only after a good rain. The grass was still wet, and puddles filled the hollow places. The girls stepped carefully around the muddy areas to keep their shoes clean and dry. They met Word just as he was dismounting to let his horse drink from Seeking Lake.

"Word," began Heart, as soon as the greetings were over, "We made a mistake yesterday and ended up in Egypt. We're sorry and we want to do it right today. We want to begin by hiding your message in our memories. So, we've come to hear what you have to say to us."

"Good!" Word smiled his approval. "I do have a message for you today and it will help you as you gather treasure. Here is my message, 'Love your enemies and do good to them, not hoping for them to return good to you. If you do this you will find much treasure and you shall be like the King, for he is kind to those who are unthankful and wicked' ... but I do also have a warning." He turned his gaze on Lily, and she could feel him looking right through her. Solemnly he said, "The treasure got through a lying tongue will not last."

Lily could feel her face burn. Surely Word could not know that she had lied to her mother that morning. That twinge of guilt pulled harder at her, but she pushed it aside, convincing herself that she had meant no harm. It was, after all, for a good purpose.

The girls repeated to themselves what Word had said, until they were sure they would not forget it. As they continued on their way, they discussed Word's message.

"Doing good to our enemies will help us find treasure," mused Heart out loud. "But I don't think I have any enemies. Do you?"

"I don't think so," said Sally, thinking hard.

The three girls were lost in thought for some time as they walked along the pleasant meadow path, wondering who Word had meant by 'enemies'.

A sudden loud shout, close behind them, made the girls jump. Whirling around, they saw two boys showing off on their dirt bikes.

"They sure think they're smart!" scoffed Lily.

Wheeling their bikes around, the boys made another pass, closer this time to the girls, and purposely slamming on their brakes in the middle of a large mud puddle, sending a spray of muddy water all over the girls. The boys howled with glee at the sight of the girls scowling angrily as they sputtered, spitting dirty water from their mouths.

"Ugh!" the girls shrieked, looking down at their splattered clothes and soaked shoes. The boys enjoyed the girl's discomfort immensely, and turned as if to ride away, but instead came up from behind to spray them yet again with the muddy water before the girls could jump out of the way.

Heart Longing and the Treasure Keys

"What horrid, horrid boys you are!" shouted Heart, glaring after them as they rode away, still laughing.

"Even my hair is full of mud!" said Lily disgustedly.

"What are we going to do?" whined Sally. "Our day is ruined; we can't search for treasure looking like this. I can't even walk!"

Heart and Lily burst out laughing as Sally tried to walk, keeping her arms and legs stiff. Then it was Sally's turn to laugh.

"You both look like you have masks on," she gasped, between burst of giggles.

"Do you think you look any better?" demanded Lily, grimacing.

"Come on girls," invited Heart. "Let's go back to my place and get cleaned up. We'll have to put off our treasure hunt until later."

The girls regretfully headed back to Heart's house, wishing they didn't have to waste time they could have spent searching for treasure.

The mud was drying in the warm morning sun, making their clothes and skin feel stiff and uncomfortable. They brushed off as much as possible, but it sure would feel good to get washed up and into some clean clothes. They were about halfway to Heart's house, when they heard someone shouting.

"HELP! HELP!" The cries pierced the air, and the girls stood still. Looking around, they could see no one, but the desperate cries continued. "Help!! Please, somebody, HELP!"

"Where are the voices coming from?" asked Lily, puzzled. Where they stood, the sounds seemed to echo back and around, making it difficult to determine from what direction they came.

"They seem to be coming from over there," decided Heart, pointing to where the meadow was interrupted by a dense growth of trees and underbrush.

As the girls hurried toward the forest, the cries for help became louder and clearer. Entering the forest, they stumbled upon a narrow path so overgrown it was difficult to follow. The overhanging branches slapped at their faces, and the low brush scratched their legs, but they took little notice. They had not gone far along the path, when suddenly the voices seemed to be coming from below them.

"Stop! Don't come any closer!" called a boy's voice. "Or you'll fall over too."

Being warned, the girls moved forward cautiously until they realized that they were on the edge of a sharp incline, so well hidden by the wide trees and thick shrubs that it was almost impossible to detect before that last step tumbled an unsuspecting hiker over the edge.

With a secure hold on a tree branch, and Sally holding tightly to her waistband, Heart leaned forward to look down the cliff wall. Some distance from the top edge, she saw two boys precariously balanced on a narrow rock ledge with only a root to grasp hold of. With a gasp she recognized the boys as being the same ones who had tormented them just a short time before. The boys looked up, eager to welcome their would-be rescuers, but when they saw Heart's face looking down on them one of the boys groaned. "Oh, no! It's those girls we splashed with mud. They'll never help us. Whatever are we to do? No one else will pass this way for ages!"

"Don't worry!" Heart shouted down to the boys. "We'll get you out. Are either of you hurt?"

"I've hurt my ankle; I think it's broken," answered one of the boys.

"Okay. We'll be back soon. Hang on!" encouraged Heart, as she moved back carefully from the edge of the cliff.

"How are we going to get them up?" asked Lily.

"I sure wish one of our Dads was home, but I know they aren't, so we'll have to think of something ourselves," said Heart.

"We need a rope," suggested Sally. "We could tie it to that tree over there." She pointed to a strong thick trunk not far away. "Then, if we threw the rope down to the boys, maybe they could climb up."

"Good idea," agreed Heart. "I think that would work. I know where my Dad keeps a long, strong rope."

And so it was agreed. Sally would wait with the boys, and Lily and Heart would go back to Heart's house. Lily and Heart ran all the way, stopping only when they reached Heart's front yard. Heart had been hoping that Trouble-Free would be home, but the house was empty.

"Fill this container with water, Lily," instructed Heart," and I'll get the rope from the garage." Heart soon returned with a thick coil of rope, and the two girls wasted no time hurrying back to where Sally was waiting for them.

Heart called out as soon as she was within shouting distance. "We're coming, Sally. Are they still alright?"

"Yes, all's well," was Sally's answering shout.

"I'm so glad you're back," welcomed Sally, when Heart reached her, but then she continued to stare expectantly in the direction Heart had come from. "Where's Lily?" she asked finally. "Didn't she come back with you?"

"Of course, she's right behind me," assured Heart, but when she turned back expecting to see Lily, she could not see her anywhere, and the forest was silent.

"That's funny," she said, thoroughly puzzled. "She was with me a minute ago. I'm sure she's alright. She must have just stopped to rest or tie her shoelace or something. She'll probably come around those trees any minute." Heart spoke confidently, but there was a vague uneasiness within her. She deliberately turned her attention to the problem at hand. "Good thing I carried the rope. Here, Sally, help me tie this end to that tree. Let's get the boys rescued."

They took the rope and tied it securely around the tree trunk. Heart was glad Trouble-Free had taught her how to tie a strong slip-proof knot.

Calling instructions down to the boys, Heart lowered the rope slowly down the cliff wall, watching to make sure it did not catch on any protruding rocks or branches. She breathed a sigh of relief when she saw the rope safely in the boys' grasp.

"Can you climb up?" asked Heart anxiously.

"I'm coming up," called the boy who wasn't hurt. "Then when I'm up I'll help my friend since he can't use his hurt foot."

Heart Longing and the Treasure Keys

He grabbed firmly onto the rope and climbed easily to the top of the cliff, while Heart and Sally both helped to pull him to safety.

"Man!" he exclaimed. "What a relief!" He then quickly turned his attention to rescuing his friend. He tied a loop in the end of the rope before he threw it back over the cliff. He shouted down to this friend, instructing him to use the rope loop as a seat harness. The injured boy managed to get the rope around him and finally called that he was ready to come up. With all three children pulling as hard as they could, and the injured boy helping as best he could with his good leg, he was soon safely on solid ground with the rest.

Exhausted, they sat leaning their backs against a fallen log. *It sure would be nice,* Heart thought, *if Lily was there with that cold jug of water. It would be so welcome in quenching their thirst. Where in the world could she be?* She still was nowhere in sight.

"I guess I should introduce us." The boy with the hurt ankle interrupted her thoughts. "I'm Tim Tough and this is my cousin Jim Rough. Uh, we didn't really deserve your help," he added sheepishly. "We had that fall coming to us. We're sorry we were so mean to you."

"That's okay," assured Heart and Sally, quick to forgive them. "We're glad we could help you. We better get you to a doctor, Tim. Your ankle looks pretty sore and swollen."

Tim could not put any weight on his ankle at all, so with Jim on one side and Heart and Sally taking turns on the other side they managed to half-carry, half-support him down the path to Heart's home. From there the boys called Tim's father, who arrived shortly to pick them up.

When the boys were gone, Sally looked at Heart, a worried frown creasing her forehead. "I'm worried about Lily," she said. "We didn't see any trace of her. Where could she have gone?"

"Could she have gone home for some reason?" wondered Heart. "Let's go check"

The girls had almost reached Lily's house, when they met Trouble-Free on his way home.

"Hey, Heart," he called," I met Pride today, and he said that he saw Lily in Egypt. What were you girls doing there?"

"Nothing at all!" exclaimed Heart, surprised by Trouble-Free's revelation. "We weren't in Egypt, or even close to it. Pride couldn't have seen Lily there."

"Well, he insisted he did," answered Trouble-Free. "He said something about her carrying a jug of water."

Heart and Sally looked at one another in dismay.

"What are we going to do? Why ever would she go to Egypt? How will we get her out?" worried Sally out loud.

"I don't know," admitted Heart, a lump rising in her throat. She swallowed. This was no time to cry. They had to think hard; Lily needed them. "We could go back along the WAY PROVIDED we took to get out of Egypt and see if we can find her," she suggested. The girls looked at one another, remembering what it was like being lost in Egypt. They really didn't want to go back.

"We have to try," said Sally firmly. "We can't just leave her there."

Heart Longing and the Treasure Keys

The two friends went back across the Stream of Refreshing, found the "WAY PROVIDED", and followed it back into Egypt. Things in Egypt had not changed. The old man, Mr. Regret, still sat outside his house, the merrymaking and games of chance were still going on in the streets. Loud music, noise, shouting and flashing lights created an atmosphere of confusion. People everywhere were involved in frenzied activity.

"How will we ever find her? Where do we even begin to look?" asked Heart, feeling rather helpless.

"We'll find her," insisted Sally bravely. "We just HAVE to."

As they passed through the streets, they were jostled, yelled at, and coaxed to come join in the games, but Heart and Sally stayed close together, ignoring everything but what they had come for – finding their lost friend.

Something of interest had caused a group of people to gather together, and Heart and Sally heard shouting and taunting voices. They stopped, wondering what was happening, but whatever or whoever was the object of the crowd's ridicule was blocked from their view. Then, suddenly, the crowd seemed to lose interest, and they melted away toward something new that had caught their attention.

Heart and Sally gasped with shock and dismay at what they saw when the crowd parted. There in front of them was Lily. She was caught and hopelessly tangled in a web of ropes. A prisoner, unable to move.

"Lily," called Heart, "Lily Truthful, whatever happened, what are you doing here?"

Lily was crying. "Oh, why did you come? And don't call me Lily Truthful, I am Lily Liar."

"No, no, the King changed your name, remember? He changed it to Lily Truthful!" cried Heart.

"Yes," answered Lily sadly, "but I lied again. I lied this morning to my mother. I lied to you and I didn't listen to Word's warning about the treasure that is got through lying would not last. I got lost when I was following you back to help the boys and now I'm so tangled up in this web, I'll never get out. Go back before you get caught here too." Lily began to sob so hard she could say no more.

"We'll not leave you!" insisted Heart and Sally loyally. "We will find a way to free you."

They tried to pull the cords of the web away from Lily but, they could not budge them. Lily was caught tight.

There must be a way! thought Heart desperately. *Oh King, please help us, please help Lily. She is sorry. She knows she has done wrong. Please forgive her and help us!*

The prayer had but formed in her mind, when it was as though Heart was again standing at the cross at the time Lily had met the King, and she heard the King's words, "You will be tempted to lie again but remember I am truth and I have given you my truth belt. When you are tempted to lie, touch your truth belt."

"Lily," cried Heart excitedly, "do you remember what the King said to you when he gave you your truth belt?"

"Yes, I remember, I haven't been able to get it out of my mind. He said to touch my truth belt when I was tempted, but

I didn't. I went ahead and lied anyway, and now it's too late. I'm so sorry!"

"Wait, Lily, please don't cry," begged Heart. "It's never too late if you are sorry! I'm sure of it. Try it now! Touch your truth belt."

Lily struggled to get one arm free to reach her belt. Heart and Lily held their breath as Lily finally had one hand free enough to reach out toward her truth belt. Stretching, she was just able touch it. The instant she touched it, she was free!

The girls shouted for joy, and Heart grabbed Lily's one hand and Sally grabbed the other as together they ran out of Egypt.

Sally and Heart both had new keys on their cords. Keys to the treasure for "LOVING YOUR ENEMIES" and also for the treasure of "HIDING WORD'S MESSAGES" in their memories.

Lily was sorry she did not have new keys, but she was thankful that she had friends who cared enough to come rescue her when she was in trouble. She was thankful too, for the valuable lesson she had learned. She knew now that nothing was worth telling a lie for. The next time she was tempted to speak other than the truth, she would touch her truth belt, remember that King Vine always spoke the truth, and that he would help her to be strong and never tell a lie again.

CHAPTER 4

"The King's Memory Book"

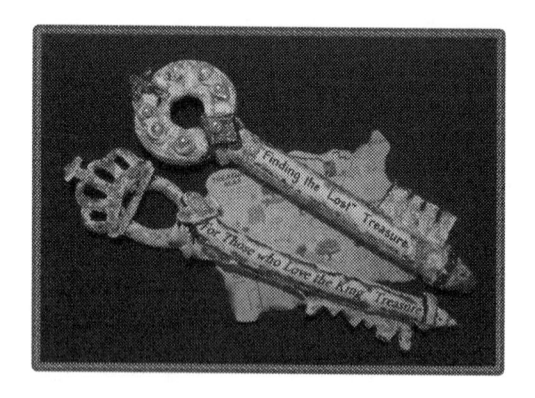

Heart sat hugging her knees in her favourite spot on top of Promise Mountain. From her vantage point, she had a perfect view of Eternal Palace. She was spending the day alone, without her friends. Sally Self-Less and her parents had gone out of town to visit her grandmother. Lily had confessed to her mother the lies she had told and was now cheerfully enduring the consequences of her disobedience – three days of extra chores. Lily felt sorry when the paper reported that except for

Heart Longing and the Treasure Keys

the weeds found in part of Lily's mother's garden, she would have won the coveted prize for having the best garden.

Heart didn't mind being alone. She loved to sit, uninterrupted, and let her imagination fill her thoughts with what it was like in Eternal Palace. She felt so close to King Vine here, as she thought about living there with him forever. She caught her breath with the thought that it wasn't just her imagination. It was really, really true! One day, Eternal Palace WOULD be her home. Her grandmother was already there. Did she know that her granddaughter, Heart, loved King Vine too and was waiting for him to call her to Eternal Palace one day? Heart wondered, oh what would it be like, spending that first day in Eternal Palace.

She felt before she saw, the warm light that fell over her. She turned her head to see Word approaching.

"I thought I would find you here," greeted Word, coming up over the last high knoll. He was leading his horse, who whinnied a soft greeting when he saw Heart.

"Oh Word, I'm so glad you are here," smiled Heart, getting up to pat the horse's nose. "There is so much I want to know about Eternal Palace. Will you tell me more about it? Who lives there, besides King Vine?"

"Eternal Palace belongs to King Vine and his Father. They have always lived there with many servants and messengers who love to do their bidding," replied Word.

"I didn't know King Vine had a Father. What is he like?" asked Heart in surprise.

"King Vine's Father is just like King Vine. To know one is to know the other. And just like King Vine, his Father also knows and loves you."

"He does?" asked Heart, her voice rising in amazement. "But I've never seen his Father."

"No," explained Word, "no one here in Eternal City has ever seen his Father. He does not leave the Eternal Palace. He lives in brilliant light, so brilliant and strong that if he were to appear to you, you would die. But, he can see you. Though he lives in Eternal Palace, he fills all things. He is all-knowing, all-seeing and all-powerful. But even though he is so great, he is interested in you and loves you even as King Vine loves you. The King's Presence that you feel around you is also the Father's Presence."

Word paused, then softly continued, "Heart, it is the Father that sent King Vine to die for you to make it possible for you to become a citizen of Eternal City. He rose from the dead, conquering death, so that you could one day go to live in Eternal Palace. There you will see and enjoy things too wonderful for you to imagine."

"Tell me more," begged Heart. "I love to hear how King Vine and his Father love me. It makes me feel so warm inside. Do they really know everything I do?"

"Yes, of course they do," answered Word. "They know you are sitting here, thinking about them."

"Do they really?" questioned Heart, staring at Eternal Palace as if maybe she might see someone looking back at her.

Heart Longing and the Treasure Keys

"It pleases them so much to see you thinking and talking about them, that they do something very special."

"What do they do?" asked Heart with great interest.

"In Eternal Palace is a beautiful book. It is called the Memory Book. When someone in Eternal City thinks and talks about the King and His Father, it is commanded that the book be opened and their names recorded."

"Really?" Heart had to know. "Do you suppose MY name is written in it?" she asked.

"Yes, I know that it is! In fact," confided Word with a smile, "I saw your name written in it just this morning."

"Oh," Heart let out a delighted sigh. She tried to imagine what her name would look like, written in the Palace Memory Book. She was sure the ink would be pure gold, and the pages would be pressed rose petals of the most delicate pink hue. The cover would be exquisitely fashioned with mother-of-pearl set with diamonds and precious stones.

After a long pause, Heart asked, "Word, you know King Vine very well, don't you?"

"Yes, dear Heart, I know him very well. I say only those things that I have heard him say and I go only where he sends me. I live in his Presence."

"That must be why I love you so!" exclaimed Heart, impulsively, with deep feeling. "You help me to know and love the King and his Father. Thank you, Word."

Heart sat for a long time after Word had ridden away, just drinking in the beauty around her and hiding deep inside her the things Word had told her.

Finally, taking a deep breath she rose, and with a long backward look at the Palace, turned to wind her way back down the mountain path.

Soft breezes played with her hair and tall grasses tickled her ankles as she walked. She was almost at the foot of Promise Mountain before she noticed something in her pocket. A key! Word must have slipped it into her pocket before he left. A key to more treasure! Heart hung it with the others around her neck and ran the rest of the way home. She hoped she wouldn't be too late. She had promised to stay with her sister, Miss Favor, while her mother ran some errands.

She burst into the house calling, "Mom, Mom! I'm home!"

"I'm here, Heart," answered her mother. "In the kitchen!"

Heart slipped to her mother's side, giving her a hug. "I'm not late, am I?" she asked.

"No, dear," assured her mother. "You are just in time. I have a few minutes before I have to leave." She looked up to smile at her daughter. "Is that a new key around your neck?"

"Yes, Mom, but I don't quite understand what treasure it unlocks."

"Well, let's have a look at your treasure map. Do you have it with you?" asked Mrs. Longing-Fulfilled.

"Yes, it's right here," said Heart pulling it from her pocket. She spread it out on the kitchen counter. Heart and her mother leaned over to study it.

"Where were you this morning, Heart?" questioned her mother.

Heart Longing and the Treasure Keys

"On top of Promise Mountain. Word told me such neat things about King Vine and his Father."

"That explains the key then," said Mrs. Longing, putting her finger on the map. "See, here the map shows treasure at the top of the mountain. A sign reads, 'TREASURE FOR THOSE WHO LOVE THE KING'. You were loving the King and thinking about him. Therefore you have treasure laid away for you."

"Isn't it exciting, Mom?" asked Heart. "Knowing we have treasure laid away for us in Eternal Palace?"

"Yes, dear," agreed her mother, with a hug. "It is very exciting indeed."

Mrs. Longing-Fulfilled picked up her sweater and purse.

"I'm off, dear Heart. In half an hour or so, you need to go pick up Miss Favor. She is at the Abiders' playing with Little Lamb. When you come back home, would you please peel the potatoes in the sink and put them on the stove? I should be home in time to finish preparing dinner."

"Okay, Mom," promised Heart.

Heart set out for the Abider home soon after her mother left. She had not been at the Abiders' for some time and she missed them. It would be nice to talk with Mrs. Abider and Star Light.

Mrs. Abider's front door was open and Heart poked her head in.

"Hello?" she called. "Is anyone home?"

"Heart," Mrs. Abider greeted her warmly. "How nice! Come on in."

"Star Light!" she called. "Heart is here!"

Star Light came in from the patio with a book in her hand.

The girls were happy to see each other and were soon absorbed in a lively conversation about the things they had experienced and learned from Word since they had last seen each other. The time went by quickly, but when the wall clock suddenly struck four, Heart knew she must go.

"OH!" she exclaimed jumping to her feet. "I've got to go. Where is Miss Favor?"

"She's in the back yard with Little Lamb," said Star Light. "I'll go call her."

She went to the patio door and looked out. "They are not here, Heart!" she called back in a puzzled tone of voice.

Star Light and Heart ran outside, searching everywhere for the two children. They were nowhere to be found and fear and dread swelled like a balloon inside them.

"Mom, the kids are gone!" shouted Star Light, almost in tears, as she ran back into the house.

"They can't be too far away," reasoned her mother calmly. "I'll stay here in case they come back. You and Heart search the neighbourhood."

Heart and Star Light looked behind heavy gates, under patios, in storage sheds. They even searched under the spreading juniper bushes in the vacant lot down the street. They called and called but no one answered.

Some distance from the Abider home was a dense forest, called the Forest of Distraction and both girls looked at it apprehensively.

Heart Longing and the Treasure Keys

"They wouldn't, would they?" asked Heart, voicing the dreaded question that was also in Star Light's mind.

"I sure hope not," answered Star Light slowly, "Little Lamb knows he is not to go near that forest. He's not even allowed out of the yard without permission."

"But they are nowhere else," argued Heart anxiously. "We must find them!"

The girls walked to the edge of the forest and called as loudly as they could, but only an ominous silence answered. They stood staring into the densely treed forest, knowing how easy it was to get lost venturing even a short distance into it.

Then, Star Light put her hand into her pocket and brought out a ball of string.

"I think this is just what we need," Star Light said. Seeing Heart's look of surprise, she explained. "I was helping them tie string to a kite. I'm glad I was too involved in my book to take the time to put the string away and I just dropped it into my pocket. It will really come in handy now to guide us back out of the forest. It is so easy to get lost in there."

As she spoke, she tied one end of the red ball of string to a tree standing on the edge of the forest, and as they began walking into the dense growth of the forest, she began to unwind the ball.

They walked deeper and deeper into the forest, calling the names of the little lost ones.

"Miss Favor! Little Lamb!" Over and over they called, then stopped to listen, but heard nothing other than the sound of their own feet on the forest floor.

Julianna Joy Klassen

The ball of string was almost used up, and Star Light and Heart knew they dared not go much farther. Hope was dying within them, and a gripping fear was almost choking them.

Heart suddenly stopped, and held out her hand to keep Star Light from walking into her.

"Star Light," she said, "let's stop for a moment. We've forgotten that the King's Presence is never far away. King Vine has not forgotten us, and he will surely help us if we ask him."

"You are right, of course," agreed Star Light, feeling ashamed that she let her fear overwhelm her. "The King knows where Little Lamb and Miss Favor are. We need not fear."

As the girls stood quietly together thinking about King Vine, their fear melted.

"Listen!" whispered Heart, and both girls strained their ears to listen. Yes! There was a faint cry.

"Miss Favor!! Little Lamb!!" They shouted, cupping their hands to their mouths. There was now no doubt! They could hear answering cries.

The girls called again. "Come this way! Come toward our voices! Keep walking!" They kept calling, and the answering voices came louder and clearer, until they heard glad shouts and the sound of little feet running over twigs and leaves.

Miss Favor and Little Lamb were gathered into eager outstretched arms and given tight hugs.

"Why did you go into the Forest of Distraction, Little Lamb?" scolded Star Light, but her voice was not angry; she was too relieved to have found him safe and sound. "You know you are not allowed to go there!"

"It was my fault," confessed Miss Favor. "Little Lamb saw a little rabbit hop past his yard, and he wanted to pet it, so I said I would catch it for him. We almost caught it, but then it ran into the forest. We were just going to go a little way, but then we lost sight of the rabbit and when we wanted to go back home we found that we were lost. We were so scared!" Her voice and lips quivered, as big tears welled up in her eyes.

"There, there," comforted Star Light and Heart lovingly. "It's all right now, you are found and I'm sure you have learned your lesson. Come now, let's go home."

The little ones, quickly forgetting the terror of being lost, thought it was great fun to follow the red string out of the forest and were soon laughing and taking turns leading the way.

Heart and Star Light did not forget their frightening experience as quickly, and they followed more slowly.

"We can't forget to thank King Vine for helping us find them," reminded Heart, "and thank him for keeping them safe."

"Yes!" agreed Star Light, and as the two girls paused for a moment to express their gratitude to the King, they felt his Presence surround them.

When Heart and Miss Favor were leaving to go home, Star Light pointed to Heart's chain. "You have another key!" she smiled.

"And so do you," laughed Heart pointing in turn to Star Light's chain.

When she got home she quickly peeled the potatoes and put them on the stove to cook. She glanced out onto the veranda to make sure Miss Favor was safely occupied with her doll and kitten. Heart pulled out her map to see where the newest treasure had come from. It was not hard to find. Not far from the Forest of Distraction, was another sign post reading, "TREASURE FOR FINDING THE LOST".

Heart had never dreamed there was so much hidden treasure in Eternal City. She smiled as she imagined how much treasure was beginning to fill her treasure chest in Eternal Palace.

CHAPTER 5

"A Voice Not Seen"

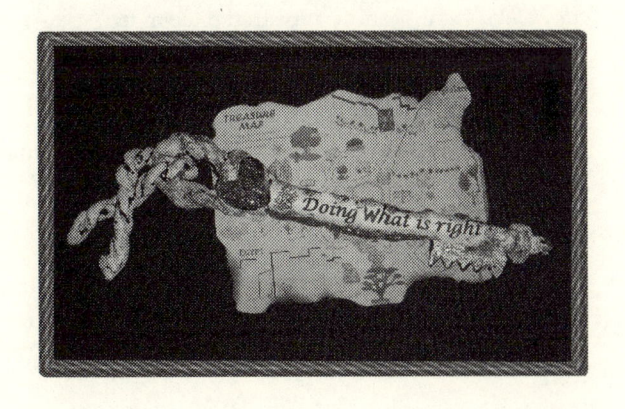

The Longing-Fulfilled family was lingering at the kitchen table having enjoyed a waffle breakfast one lazy Saturday morning.

"Trouble-Free," observed his father, "you are very quiet this morning. What have you planned for today?"

"Nothing," was the glum reply. "My friends are all busy and I have no one to spend the day with."

"Hey," said Heart cheerfully, "my friends are all busy too. Would you like to go treasure hunting with me?"

Trouble-Free brightened, "Weeell, that would be alright, I guess," he answered, trying not to sound too excited at the idea of spending a day with a girl, even if she was his sister.

"Me too, me too," insisted Miss Favor.

Her smile disappeared behind a frown when she saw her mother shaking her head. To ward off anything more threatening, Mrs. Longing-Fulfilled said quickly, "I need you to hunt treasure with me. I wouldn't find any if you didn't help me!"

Miss Favor's sunny smile appeared once more. "Okay," she agreed. "I'll hunt treasure with you, Mommy."

Mr. Longing-Fulfilled turned to Trouble-Free and Heart. "So, it's settled then. Where are you planning to search today?"

"We don't know," answered Heart, glancing at Trouble-Free. "We'll have to spend some time studying our map."

"Good, just make sure you stay where it is safe and listen to Word. I don't want you getting lost or hurt," advised Mr. Longing-Fulfilled in a fatherly tone.

"We won't," promised Trouble-Free easily. "Come on, Heart. Aren't you ready yet?"

"Yes, I'm ready!" Heart quickly tied her last shoelace and followed Trouble-Free out the door.

Not far from the Longing-Fulfilled home, they met Word astride his big horse. He waved a friendly greeting.

"Where are you off to today?" he asked.

"We haven't decided yet," answered Heart. "Do you have any directions for us?"

"The right doers and they that sow righteousness shall find a great treasure," quoted Word, as if he had the answer waiting before they asked.

Heart repeated the words in her mind, trying to make sense of them. Her brother asked the question in her mind, "How do we know when we are sowing righteousness?"

"Love your neighbour as yourself and you will always do right. Listen carefully and you will hear," was Word's somewhat puzzling reply and with a smile he was gone.

"Did you understand what he said, Heart?" asked Trouble-Free. "I didn't."

"No," admitted Heart thoughtfully, "not exactly, but I always try to remember what he said because sooner or later it suddenly becomes clear to me."

They repeated Word's messages over and over until they had them memorized. They pulled out their treasure maps but for some reason found it difficult to concentrate. Trouble-Free gave up and let his mind wander to other things.

"I wonder what this treasure sign here means," mused Heart. "It says 'Doing What is Right'".

When Trouble-Free did not answer she looked up at him. He was staring off into space.

"Trouble-Free!" scolded Heart, feeling annoyed with her brother. "You are not paying attention!"

"I was looking at that tree over there," answered Trouble-Free, choosing not to respond to the frustration in Heart's voice and the frown on her face. "It's a terrific tree for a fort hide-away. You want to help me build one?" Heart stared at him for a long moment.

"Oh, alright," she gave in with a sigh. It was no good searching for treasure alone and anyway, she had never built a fort before. It might just be fun!

As they neared the tree, Trouble-Free let out a sharp whistle! "Just look at this, Heart!" he said, pointing. Half overgrown by underbrush lay supplies perfect for building a tree fort. "Someone else must have had the same idea I had and then for some reason abandoned the idea. What a good deal for us!" Then looking up into the tree they saw that the floor of the fort had already been laid.

It appeared that someone had made plans for a fort, gathered the material, started it and then for some reason abandoned the project before it was finished - or - could it be that someone had purposely left it all for them to find? Trouble-Free sorted through the wood, rope and twine lying in the half-hidden pile and declared that there was more than enough to finish the fort. There was even a ladder so they could climb up to where the fort would be built.

At first Trouble-Free took charge and gave directions on how to put the fort together, but soon Heart was as involved as Trouble-Free and even offered some opinions of her own.

" Hey, Trouble-Free, if we put up a wall here with a window opening it would look out over that fragrant magnolia tree, and then even when the tree isn't blooming we could still see that pretty little field where the flowers bloom all summer."

"Forget it," disagreed Trouble-Free. "I've planned to put the wall with an opening on this side over-looking that ravine. Then I can pretend I'm a watchman on the wall of a city, ready to warn the people when danger approaches."

Heart thought flowers were prettier to look at than the ravine and said so. Trouble-Free responded with a remark about it being silly to sit in a fort and look at flowers. One insult led to another until their argument escalated into a name calling shouting match.

"Trouble-Free!"

Trouble-Free jumped, and looked around to see who had spoken his name so loudly. The voice was not familiar and as he looked around, he could see no one other than Heart.

"What's the matter with you?" asked Heart sharply, when Trouble-Free suddenly fell silent and looked at her strangely.

"Did you hear someone call my name?" he asked.

"Of course not," scoffed Heart. "There is no-one here but us and how could you possibly hear anyone when you are shouting so loud! Stop trying to change the subject and don't be silly. It won't make me let you have the window on that side."

"Well, I won't have it on the other side," argued Trouble-Free stubbornly.

"TROUBLE-FREE!"

The voice was louder this time, leaving no doubt that Trouble-Free had indeed heard someone call him.

The voice seemed to have come from above him and looking up, Trouble-Free saw a bird sitting on a branch. It was not a strikingly beautiful bird, but there was something fascinating about it – even compelling. Trouble-Free stared at it.

"Who or what are you?" he asked, ignoring the fact that birds do not usually talk.

"I am Conscience," replied the bird, his black eyes very piercing. "I have been sent by the King to help you."

"Help me?" asked Trouble-Free, feeling rather silly to be having a conversation with a bird.

"Why are you talking to the tree?" scoffed Heart. "It can't hear you, you know."

"I'm not talking to the tree," Trouble-Free quickly defended himself, before he realized that the truth would sound no less silly than him talking to a tree. "There's a bird in the tree. Its name is Conscience."

"A bird, Trouble-Free?" laughed Heart. "You were talking to a bird? Are you sure you are feeling alright?"

"There IS a bird in the tree," insisted Trouble-Free, stoutly. "It's right over there." He pointed to the branch leaning over toward them. Heart followed his pointing finger.

"There is no bird," said Heart, losing patience with her brother.

"Yes, there is! It's right over there!" Trouble-Free pointed triumphantly to the bird that seemed to him to be in plain sight. But even as he pointed, he realized he was suddenly pointing to a branch with nothing on it but ordinary leaves. He began to feel a little foolish.

"Well, there WAS a bird," he insisted lamely, trying to save face. He turned the conversation back to their argument.

"It's a much better idea to put the window over here. After all, boys know more about forts than girls do, and it WAS my idea to build it."

"Girls always know better where windows should go," countered Heart quickly, still determined to have it her way. "I know it should go here."

"Well, I should never have asked you to help me. You're no help at all." He was thinking girls were useless and dumb, and was about to tell Heart so, when again he heard the voice.

"TROUBLE-FREE!"

The voice this time carried such authority that Trouble-Free dared not ignore it, though he wished he could. Slowly, he looked up into the tree - would he see the bird again? Or an empty branch? But yes, there it sat again, with its beady eyes looking straight at him. Trouble-Free stared back without saying a word.

"Trouble-Free!" Conscience repeated. "Don't you remember that the King changed your name from Trouble to Trouble-Free? Use the power the King has given you and make peace. Do what is right!"

Even as Trouble-Free stared in stunned silence, the bird flew away.

"Whatever are you staring at?" demanded Heart.

"Oh, nothing ... Nothing at all," answered Trouble-Free, not wanting Heart to make him feel foolish again. "Uh ... Heart," he continued, before Heart could press him further. "I was thinking, why couldn't we have two windows. Then you can enjoy your flowers and I can keep watch."

"That is a marvellous idea!" agreed Heart, relieved the quarrel was over. "You are a genius, Trouble-Free."

And so work resumed on the hide-away fort.

It was late afternoon before two weary children sat down in their completed fort. They were well pleased with their labours. Adding to the supplies left under the tree, they had tightly woven branches together with the twine to fill in the gaps in the outer walls. Pulling down long tendrils from the ivy covering the tree, they used them to outline the two windows. Heart especially loved the windows.

"Aren't they lovely?" she asked Trouble-Free. "And the ivy will just keep on growing. It was perfect that you chose a tree for our fort that already had such a nice thick vine growing up its trunk. If we train the vines carefully, soon our whole fort will be completely covered, and no-one will even know it is here."

"That will be neat," agreed Trouble-Free. "I'll make a rope ladder so we can climb up and down easily, the ladder is great but much too obvious. We can hide it again, after we have the rope ladder in place."

"But couldn't people find it same as we did?" asked Heart.

"No," Trouble-Free replied, "we can tuck it against the tree trunk behind the ivy vines. No-one will even know it's there."

It didn't take Trouble-Free long, using the knot skills he had learned at boy's camp, to craft a sturdy rope ladder that reached from the fort floor to the bottom of the tree trunk. What fun the fort was going to be. Heart and Trouble-Free eagerly made plans for the summer.

Heart Longing and the Treasure Keys

The sudden sound of voices interrupted their plans. Trouble-Free hurriedly pulled up the rope ladder, hoping whoever was coming was still too far away to have noticed. He crept to a window and cautiously looked out. Quickly, he ducked back out of sight, thankful he had already hidden the ladder against the tree trunk.

"Oh, no!" he groaned. "It's Little Lamb and Miss Favor."

"What are they doing here?" asked Heart in dismay. "They shouldn't be so far from home on their own. Maybe if we keep quiet and keep out of sight, they won't notice the fort and go home."

But it was too late. The little ones' sharp eyes had already caught sight of the fort.

"Hey, Little Lamb," shouted Miss Favor excitedly. "Just look at that neat fort. Wouldn't you like to go inside?"

"Oh yes," agreed Little Lamb. "Let's call – maybe someone is inside and will come out."

So the two began calling and shouting, "Hello, to whoever is in the fort! Can we come visit?"

Heart and Trouble-Free sat quietly in the furthest corner from the door, hoping the two little ones would give up and go home.

"Heart Longing! Trouble-Free!"

Trouble-Free instantly recognized the voice of Conscience and looking up saw him sitting in the window. He glanced at Heart, knowing better than to ask her if she saw the bird. But this time, she too, was staring at the bird.

"There really is a bird," she said with astonishment.

"I am Conscience," explained the bird again. "I am sent by the King to help you. Don't you remember what he said about loving your neighbour as yourself?"

"Yes, but Miss Favor and Little Lamb are not my neighbours." Trouble-Free tried to justify himself.

"No?" questioned Conscience. "Then who is?" and with that he flew away.

Heart and Trouble-Free looked at one another.

"I guess we'd better," they agreed, and crawling to the door they looked down on Little Lamb and Miss Favor.

"Oh! Goody, goody!" the two intruders exclaimed at the sight of Heart and Trouble-Free. "Can you help us come up too?"

In a few minutes, the four were seated comfortably on the floor of the fort. The little ones' honest amazement and admiration of the fort made Trouble-Free and Heart quite forget that they had not wanted to share the fort with anyone.

"Oh, I almost forgot," said Miss Favor suddenly. "Mom said I could bring you these if you weren't too far away." She giggled a little, knowing that they had come farther than they should have. She struggled with a package that was a tight fit in her little backpack.

"Here," she said finally managing to free the package. "I brought some fresh cookies, and water from the Stream of Refreshing."

Needless to say, the goodies were quickly consumed, enjoyed by all and no one minded that some of the cookies had broken into pieces. It was getting late, and reluctantly, the four headed for home.

Heart Longing and the Treasure Keys

Later that evening both Heart and Trouble-Free had new keys. Keys to unlock the "TREASURE FOR DOING WHAT IS RIGHT".

"It's amazing, isn't it," commented Heart to Trouble-Free, as she was looking at her map before saying good-night, "how easy it is to find treasure when you are not really looking for it. The important thing is to remember all of Word's messages."

"Yes," agreed Trouble-Free. Heart added, "And when we are willing to give in and do something nice for someone else, it makes us feel good. And, when we do right, others are encouraged to do right as well."

"So true, "said Trouble-Free with a yawn. "And I guess we need to be thankful for Conscience too, he's quite helpful. Good-night, Heart. Today was fun!"

CHAPTER 6

"The Plot"

Just inside the wall of Egypt, behind the Rock of Bondage, Tom Thief, Darcy Deceit and Pride sat in a circle, their heads together, earnestly discussing a matter of seeming great importance.

"Look," Tom Thief was saying, "I've asked you to meet me here because Mr. Destroyer has hired me to do something for him, and I need you to help me. You know Heart Longing-Fulfilled?" It was more a statement than a question. He paused. Both Darcy and Pride nodded.

Heart Longing and the Treasure Keys

"Yah," they said. There was no love in their voices. "We know her."

"Good," continued Tom. "Then you know she has been gathering Eternal Treasure. Well ..." He said, leaning forward to emphasize his next words. "We are going to steal her treasure!" He watched with smug satisfaction as his words had their desired effect. Slowly, there spread over Darcy and Pride's faces an ugly expression of glee as they imagined what they could do to harm Heart. They leaned forward eagerly to hear Tom's plan.

"Great idea, Tom! But how are we going to do it? You know the King always has his protection around her. He'll never let anyone intending to harm her get close to her," objected Pride.

"Right, unless we lead her away to where that protection cannot reach her. There are ways," said Tom knowingly. "Mr. Destroyer has taught me several. We shall steal her treasure before the day is over."

"Good!" exclaimed both Darcy and Pride. "Count us in, and tell us your plan."

"Okay, here's what we'll do." Tom Thief laid out his plan carefully, making sure that each of them understood their part. They could not, would not, fail! What a satisfying coup it would be to steal Heart's treasure! All three were smug with confidence that the deed would be done.

Meanwhile, Heart was just finishing her breakfast and was totally unaware of the sinister plot being laid against her that very moment.

She was, following her morning habit, pouring over her map on the kitchen table. She traced the way she had already gone, smiling as she thought of each of the treasure keys she had already found at the various places marked on the map. Her finger passed where she had been the day before. A little frown creased her forehead as she bent to study the map closer. The path there seemed to diverge in several directions. Two of the paths were marked with warnings. One read "Beware of the Thief" and the other read "Be not Deceived" and then a tiny marker indicated treasure identified as "TO AN OVERCOMER, THE MORNING STAR".

Heart drew a deep breath of anticipated pleasure. *The Morning Star – what a beautiful sounding treasure! Oh, if only she could find it today.*

"Heart," Mrs. Longing-Fulfilled broke into Heart's concentration, as she came into the room and smiled at Heart pouring over her map. "I'm always happy to see you studying your treasure map. Do you know what treasure you will be searching for today?"

"The Morning Star treasure," sighed Heart, her eyes shining.

"Sounds beautiful," agreed her mother. "I'm sorry to interrupt your map study, but I promised Mrs. Servant this recipe for preserves. She needs it today, and I just don't have time to bring it to her. Will you drop it off for me on your way?"

"Sure," responded Heart willingly. "It will be a nice walk and maybe even on my way to finding treasure. I'll take the long way around. It's a more interesting path."

A worried look crossed Mrs. Longing-Fulfilled's face. "Maybe it's more interesting, but it's also more dangerous. If you go that way, stick to the path and be extra careful."

Neither Heart nor her mother saw Tom Thief's face at the window, listening to their conversation. He laughed with soundless mirth. This was going to be even easier than he had expected.

"Oh, I'll be careful," promised Heart. "It's such a beautiful sunny day. What could happen to me?"

Mrs. Longing-Fulfilled smiled at her daughter but cautioned her once more. "Just be careful. Here is the recipe. Mind you don't lose it."

Heart tucked it carefully into her pocket and started on her way. She loved the caressing warmth of the sun on her bare skin. The air was fresh and clean, and the path she followed led her through her favourite meadow covered in a profusion of wild flowers like a palette of colour.

Each little flower seemed to smile and nod a greeting to her while the grasses ever so gently waved their long arms. Heart stopped to watch. It was as if the whole field was listening to a heavenly symphony, and as wave after wave of melody floated across their heads, the flowers and grasses moved united in their response of praise. Lost in the rhythm of such harmony, Heart could feel herself being caught up into it too. If only she could hear what they heard!

She walked as slowly as she could through the meadow, wanting to enjoy it for as long as she could, but all too soon she could see the path taking her beyond where the flowers bloomed. Unless ... Heart stopped and looked thoughtfully at a narrow trail leading off from the main well-trodden path. If she took that trail that stayed closer to the meadow, she was sure that it joined the main path again higher up. Her mother had warned her about staying on the main path, but this was just a small detour, surely there could be no harm in it. Heart took the side path, not noticing a shadow fall over the path. The boy to whom the shadow belonged, had been following her, and he rubbed his hands gleefully when he saw her leave the main path.

For a time, the path wound gently among the rainbow hued field of flowers, and Heart was glad she had taken the detour. But then, suddenly without warning, the path took an abrupt turn and changed from a gentle meadow path to a rugged mountain trail. Jagged rocks and cliffs forced the path to snake its way up and around, then down and back again, to find the only possible route up and over the mountain. Heart's foot slipped several times over some loose rocks and she caught her breath sharply as she almost fell. She began to fear that she was lost and the trail a more dangerous one than she cared to be on. *Surely*, she thought, *there must be an easier path or, if not, at least there should have been a warning sign at the beginning of the trail.*

The sun was now high in the sky and beat mercilessly down on Heart. The day no longer seemed so beautiful. In fact, it had become muggy and hot with dark clouds hovering in the sky.

Heart wished she had worn something cooler. She wished she had thought to bring some refreshments. If only she could have a drink of water right now to quench her thirst! But there was no stream nor even a trickle of water in sight. If only Mrs. Servant had not asked for that silly recipe, Heart would at this very moment be somewhere cool and comfortable enjoying a nice day. Why had she agreed to deliver that stupid recipe anyway? Couldn't Mrs. Servant have picked it up herself if she wanted it so badly? This was supposed to be a day spent in finding that special treasure, but ... Look at her! Was she having fun? Hardly!

Thinking these kind of angry thoughts, Heart's steps grew slower and the frown on her face grew deeper. She was so wrapped up in her discontentment and grumbling that she walked right past the little sign reading "Self-peak Falls" without even noticing it. Tom Thief, still following at a safe distance, smiled to himself as he watched her steps become heavier and her usually happy face become darker and darker with self-pity. Then, she stopped to rest in the ME circle of grass in the park area.

Tom was so sure he had won, that he was not as careful to keep out of sight. If the drab colors of his clothes had not blended so easily into the grey of the mountain rock and dry soil, and if Heart had not been so wrapped up in herself, she would surely have noticed him. But as it was, she had no idea she was not alone. Finally, still disgruntled, she got up, straightened her shirt and continued on her way.

"Just a little farther, Heart!" Tom coaxed in a hoarse whisper. "Just a little farther and you will fall over the cliff, and then you will lose your treasure."

He clenched and unclenched his clammy hands, anticipating his victory. He could almost taste it, he was so close! But wait ... what WAS she doing now? Why did she sit down on the Leaning Bench? Tom Thief watched in dismay as he watched Heart sitting with her head in her hands.

"What IS the matter with me?" Heart cried aloud. "Why am I having such a pity party and thinking such awful thoughts. I am thinking only of me. Where did I go wrong? How I wish Word was here!"

And of course he was! His horse's neigh was a most welcome sound and covered the sounds of Tom Thief's groans of frustration.

"Oh NO!" he snarled. "She can't talk to Word! He'll spoil all my plans!!"

There was nothing he could do but watch in helpless aggravation.

"Word, help me, please," begged Heart. "I don't like the way I'm feeling. What did I do wrong?"

"You stepped off the King's path and went your own way. A way that you thought would be better. Your own way is never better, Heart. It always leads to self-thinking, and self-thinking leads to bitter thoughts and angry feelings. Beware of the root of bitterness because it will grow and bring forth fruit that will cause much pain and trouble. You are sitting on the Leaning Bench. It offers you two choices. Either you lean on your own understanding, or you lean on King Vine."

Heart knew Word was right. "Thank you, Word," she said humbly. "I will be more careful to keep to the old well-worn paths I know are right."

She sat for some time after Word was gone, thinking about what he had said. Word was right. Going her own way had filled her with grumbling thoughts that led her astray until her joy was all gone. Heart stood up. She determined to let only right thoughts lead her now. It WAS a beautiful day, and she determined to be thankful that she had opportunity to do something helpful for her mother and Mrs. Servant.

Tom watched her get up. "Good ... good ..." he thought. "Maybe, just maybe, all is not lost. Maybe she'll keep going ... if she just doesn't see that sign ...."

But he hoped in vain. Heart turned and this time, looked straight at the sign that read "Self-peak Falls". She also looked at the sign that pointed to "Selfish Park". She shook her head. How could she have been so foolish to not pay attention to where she was going?

She retraced her steps until she came to where she had turned onto the detour path. With relief she stepped back on the main path. It was good to be on the right way once again.

Tom Thief watched her, angrily scowling, because his plan had gone awry. He turned and slunk off in the other direction to find Darcy Deceit. Plan B must be put into action as quickly as possible.

Heart was now not far from Mrs. Hand's house. In fact, the little uncared for house was just coming into sight. Heart had not been to Mrs. Hand's home for a good while, but as she drew nearer she saw that everything was just as it always was – dirty, uncared for and overgrown. Mrs. Idle Hand would never change. The door suddenly opened, and as Heart watched, Mrs. Hand came out stumbling over an old flower pot left in front of the door.

"Good morning!" called Heart, wondering whether or not she should expect a return greeting. "Where are you going today?"

Mrs. Hand grunted when she saw Heart, and for a moment Heart expected Mrs. Hand to totally ignore her, but then, she said in a sharp tone of voice, "Mrs. Servant has invited me to tea. If it wasn't that I so hate to make my own tea, I wouldn't be going." Then she stopped and looked suspiciously at Heart. "What are you doing here? It surely wasn't to come see me."

"No, it wasn't," answered Heart, truthfully. Then a marvellous thought came into her head. "Mrs. Hand," she continued with more enthusiasm, "would you do me a favour? I have this recipe that Mrs. Servant needs. Seeing you are on your way to her house, would you take it with you and give it to her? It would save me some time."

Mrs. Hand pulled the corners of her mouth down into an even deeper frown. She was not in the habit of doing favours for anyone. It was far too much trouble, and besides, if she did one favour, who knows how many people would expect her to run all their errands for them. NO THANKS! But ... then she remembered what people were saying about how she had mistreated Heart. Not that she really cared what people said about her, but maybe this would be a good way to keep them quiet!

"Okay, okay," she agreed ungraciously. "But mind you, it's just this once!"

She snatched the envelope Heart held out to her, and without a backward glance or a goodbye or even acknowledging Heart's expression of gratitude, she began to move herself slowly down the path in the direction of Mrs. Servant's home.

Heart Longing and the Treasure Keys

Heart smiled to herself. If Mrs. Hand was going to walk as slowly as that, she would be arriving long after tea was over.

Heart took a deep breath, relishing her freedom! Free to enjoy the rest of the day and free to search for more treasure. Just behind Mrs. Hand's house, the path disappeared among the trees and brush that covered the little hill obscuring the view behind it. Curious to see what lay on the other side, Heart began to climb the hill. It was not a difficult climb, and before long she found herself standing at the very top of the incline. To her surprise, her vantage point commanded a full view of Egypt. She hadn't realized it was so close to Mrs. Hand's house.

"It's a fascinating view, isn't it?" asked a soft voice at her elbow.

Startled, Heart jumped and turned to see Darcy Deceit had come up behind her. "Oh," she responded flatly, a tone of welcome clearly lacking in her voice.

"I don't blame you for not being glad to see me," answered Darcy easily, reading Heart's expression. "I haven't been very nice to you, but truly, I'm sorry! I really would like to be more like you."

Heart stared hard at Darcy, not really knowing whether she was sincere or not.

"Were you on your way down?" Darcy asked nodding towards Egypt.

"Oh no!" replied Heart firmly. "I won't go down there. It's an awful place."

"I agree," answered Darcy emphatically. Heart looked at her in surprise. Maybe Darcy WAS changing, but then Darcy added. "But it can also be very nice. It really depends on how you look at it."

Heart did not answer; she only shook her head to show her disagreement.

"Really," insisted Darcy. "I was just on my way down to hear Mr. Worldly Wise speak. He is really very good! He's speaking on how to be more successful in making where you live a better place."

Heart felt a quiver of interest in spite of herself. Mr. Wise had been one of her favourite teachers back in World City. So he was still teaching. She wouldn't mind seeing him again. But not in Egypt! She would not go there, not even to hear him.

Once again, Darcy seemed to read her thoughts.

"I know how you feel about going back to Egypt," she said sympathetically, "but he's going to be speaking in an open air meeting just inside Egypt's gates. You could probably hear him if you just stood by the gate. You wouldn't even have to go inside."

Heart considered. It was tempting ... still ... she hesitated. "I don't know."

"I heard him yesterday," coaxed Darcy. "He was so good. He even encourages his listeners to consider the words of King Vine."

"He does?" asked Heart. She did not remember him ever talking about King Vine when she sat in his classes. Maybe he too, had become a follower of the King since then, In that case it would surely be alright to go hear him.

"Okay," Heart decided. "I'll come, but no further than the gate."

Heart Longing and the Treasure Keys

"Of course not," assured Darcy. Heart did not see her give a 'so far so good' signal behind her back to Pride and Tom Thief who were hidden behind a shrub not far away.

Mr. Worldly Wise had already begun speaking when Heart reached the gate. Darcy had spoken the truth. He was just inside the gate, and she could see and hear him clearly without going inside Egypt. Mr. Wise looked their way and smiled in recognition when he caught Heart's eyes on him. Heart smiled back shyly.

"Everyone has the right to have what makes him or her happy," Mr. Worldly Wise was saying. "It is a right you must defend, must stand up for. Decide what you want and go for it. Don't let anyone stop you. Don't let anyone tell you that you are wrong to covet what you desire, what you need to be satisfied. Feeling guilty is harmful, and will rob you of the strength you need to pursue your own goals. Don't let what other people think influence you. YOU decide what is right and wrong for you. Do what feels good to you. You deserve the best, it is your right – your entitlement. The world owes you happiness. Don't worry about everyone else – they'll never thank you. Think about yourself – you are number one! How do YOU feel? What do YOU want?"

Heart listened, vaguely confused. Mr. Worldly Wise's words sounded good and stirred something inside her, but why did they make her feel uncomfortable at the same time - like something was wrong about the message he was preaching.

Mr. Wise continued. "Many people like the idea of a higher power, something or someone beyond themselves. That's great!

Believe in a god, name him what you will – it will not change him. Call him Mother Earth, Power of the Universe or call him King Vine, whatever helps you plug into the universal or cosmic power that will enable you to be and get what you want and need."

An idea of a higher power? … name him anything … a way to have what she wanted… Heart was feeling more and more uncomfortable with what she was hearing.

As if Mr. Worldly Wise could read her thoughts, he said, "The image you conjure up in your mind will become reality to you just as someone else's image is reality to them."

"No!" cried Heart, not realizing she was shouting. "No! King Vine is NOT an image I conjured up in my mind. He is real! He is very real! And it DOES matter what I call him. You are wrong! You are very wrong! King Vine loves me, and I love him!"

Shaken and confused, Heart turned and ran from the sound of Mr. Worldly Wise's voice.

Darcy followed her. "Stop, Heart," she gasped. "Stop! I can't run anymore!"

Heart slowed her pace and turned slowly to look at Darcy through her tears.

"He was lying," she insisted. "He was lying, and so were you. You said he was a follower of King Vine."

"Well, I didn't say he was exactly a follower. He doesn't tell anyone NOT to follow King Vine. Anyhow," Darcy argued. "What makes you think YOU know the only way? Does everyone have to follow the King the way you do?"

Heart Longing and the Treasure Keys

Heart did not know how to answer Darcy. Why was it so hard to think clearly? Why did her thoughts all seem to be in a fog? If only Word was with her, he would surely help her. He was never confusing. Looking up, she saw Word slip out from behind a thick tree trunk where he had just tethered his horse. She searched his face knowing that, there, she would find her answers. Word looked deep into Heart's eyes, and then he gently spoke what Heart knew were the words of King Vine. "I am the Light of the world. If you follow me you will never stumble, though there be many who would confuse you by false teaching meant to lead you astray. Follow me closely, and I will shed light upon your path. I alone have the truth."

The confusion fled as Heart listened to Word, and the Presence surrounded her. King Vine WAS real, he was with her, and he had promised never to leave her. A peace enveloped Heart, and she was no longer afraid. She turned to look at Darcy and seeing the puzzled look on her face, realized that Darcy had neither seen nor heard Word's voice.

"What happened?" she asked in a strange voice.

"You wouldn't understand," replied Heart vaguely, realizing that it would be of no use to try to explain to Darcy the meaning of Word's message or even to convince her that she had just seen him. So all she would say was, "I don't care what Mr. Worldly Wise or anyone else says. I am going to believe King Vine, and I am going to follow him."

Somehow Darcy seemed to know there was no point in arguing further, and with an angry shrug of her shoulders she turned and walked quickly away.

Heart continued to walk away from Egypt. Had she looked back she may have caught sight of Pride and Tom Thief waiting for Darcy to rejoin them at Egypt's gate.

"Why did you let her go?" asked Tom accusingly, when Darcy came alongside.

"I couldn't stop her," snapped Darcy. "Something I can't explain happened. Somehow the King came to help her."

Tom Thief stared off into the distance, his mind working. Then he turned to Pride. "Okay, it's your turn now. It's our last chance. Plan C. Don't you fail too!" The three spoke together for a few minutes then Pride broke away and ran after Heart.

In a short time, Pride caught up to Heart, then slowed his steps to match hers. He walked in silence, pretending not to notice the sideways glances Heart threw his way, but she too said nothing.

Finally, Pride spoke. "Heart, I just wanted to tell you how very much I admire you."

Heart was immediately on guard. Had he been talking to Darcy? "Admire me?" she repeated, staring at Pride and wondering what kind of game he was playing.

"I'm serious," Pride insisted. "People are so easily persuaded to believe whatever they hear, and I admire you for not believing Mr. Worldly Wise. Very few see the deception in his enticing words. I think YOU are really much wiser than he is."

Heart was amazed at Pride's words. She? Wiser than Mr. Wise? Never would such a notion have occurred to her.

"Yes, you were wise enough to see that his words did not agree with King Vine's words. You made the right choice – to follow King Vine. You are really quite something, Heart."

Heart listened with astonishment. Could Pride really be talking about HER? But the more she thought about it, the more she almost believed he was right. It was true, she hadn't been taken in by Mr. Worldly Wise. She had recognized there was something wrong with what he was saying. Maybe that did, indeed, make her wiser than her old teacher.

"I don't know what you did to Darcy Deceit. No-one ever wins an argument with her," continued Pride with a sly side glance at Heart. "And yet, you just looked at her and she walked away. You've got something, Heart, what is it?"

"Do you really want to know?" Heart asked eagerly. She was beginning to almost enjoy Pride's company. He made her feel so good. She hadn't thought she had done so well that day. In fact, she had been feeling ashamed of herself for letting Darcy talk her into going to Egypt to listen to her old teacher. Yet now, listening to Pride – she could really see it in a different light.

Before Pride could answer Heart's question, someone fell in step with them, and Pride stopped to introduce his friend.

"Heart, this is Tom. Tom meet Heart."

"Heart smiled a warm greeting. She was forgetting to stay on guard – forgetting that Pride and his friends could not be trusted.

"Wow, isn't she something!" praised Tom Thief. "She is just like you said, Pride. Smart and pretty too. There is such a special glow about her!"

Heart blushed with embarrassment, but she could not deny the pleasure Tom's words gave her. She wondered why she had ever thought Pride was so awful. And his friend was really nice too. She smiled at them both.

"What a lovely collection of keys you have around your neck, Heart," admired Tom. "May I ask what they are for?"

"Oh, these are the keys that unlock my treasure," answered Heart proudly.

"Wow!" Tom and Pride both sounded duly impressed.

"You wouldn't let me look at them, would you?" requested Tom Thief slyly.

"Sure," agreed Heart, unaware of any mischief plotted against her. She slipped them from her neck, and holding them in her hand, was about to explain how she had found each one – but before she realized Tom's intent, he snatched the keys from her hand and began to run. Pride followed close on his heels, guffawing.

"NO! WAIT! Come back!" shouted Heart desperately, but even as she shouted, she knew it would do no good. Her keys were gone. She couldn't bear it. Oh, how could she have been so foolish; she saw it all so clearly now. It had all been a clever plot. Tom Thief and Pride had tricked her because they planned all along to steal her treasure keys. How could she have been so blind? She had foolishly let the words of Pride take hold in her mind, and they had blinded her to see that Tom was nothing but a thief. And now, now it was all too late … her treasure keys were gone.

"Oh, King Vine," she sobbed. "Can you ever forgive me, and if it is not too late, help me to somehow get my treasure keys back?"

Heart choked back her sobs, and in the moment's silence, she heard someone clear his throat.

Startled, she whirled about. It was Humble, leaning against a tree. He looked even smaller than she remembered, but he was a welcome sight.

"Humble," she cried. "Oh, I am so glad to see you. You are a trustworthy friend."

Humble smiled as he sprang nimbly to his feet. "Come quickly! I don't think Pride and Tom Thief are far away."

He grasped Heart's hand to hurry her along with him.

"But what can we do?" asked Heart, wondering how the two of them could overpower Pride and Tom Thief who both looked so big and strong.

Humble did not answer Heart. He seemed to know where he was going but then he stopped so short Heart almost bumped into him.

"What …" she started to ask.

"Shhh …," cautioned Humble, pointing through the bushes in front of him. There sat Darcy Deceit, Pride and Tom Thief admiring Heart's treasure keys, laughing gleefully over having successfully stolen them from Heart. "Guess she's not as good as she thought she was, huh?" Darcy sneered.

"What are we going to do?" whispered Heart, feeling it was all very hopeless. There were three of them and only Humble and her. She was not very big, and Humble was even smaller.

She certainly didn't know much about fighting, and Humble didn't look like he did either.

"Watch," commanded Humble with a little smile.

He stepped out in plain sight and the three thieves froze in surprise. Then, they moved as if to run.

"Stop right there," demanded Humble in a quiet voice. Even Heart felt that somehow that voice demanded obedience.

Pride was holding the keys, and Humble walked up to stand before him.

"Pride," Humble addressed him. Pride stared down at Humble in disbelief, as Humble continued to speak. "You may have stolen Heart's keys, but do you know where her treasure is?"

"We'll find it," boasted Pride a little uncertainly. "It can't be far away, and we have the keys to unlock it. What can stop us?" Pride put his hands on his hips and stared down at Humble trying hard not to let his friends see that he was beginning to tremble.

"Two things will stop you." Humble spoke quietly, yet firmly. "One, Heart's treasure is in Eternal Palace. You cannot break in there. Two, Heart is my friend and I will defend her. YOU are an old enemy of mine, but you know your strength is powerless before me. Give me those keys."

To Heart's utter amazement, Pride began to shrink and shrivel until Humble seemed to tower over him. Without a word he handed him the keys.

"Now go!" commanded Humble, and Heart's three enemies wasted no time in leaving, stumbling over one another in their haste.

Heart Longing and the Treasure Keys

"Humble!" cried Heart with grateful delight. "How can I ever thank you enough. You got my keys back!"

Humble hung the keys around her neck and said, "Guard them carefully, dear Heart. Hold fast to what is good. Do not keep company with Tom Thief, do not let Darcy Deceit blind you, and do not let Pride's words take hold in your mind. They will steal the keys to your treasure. And always remember, I am your friend, and I am much stronger than I look," he added with a wink.

Tears of joy swam in Heart's eyes as she smiled her thanks at Humble. He lifted his hand in a wave and was gone.

It was late. Heart knew she must hurry home. Glancing down as she began to walk, her eyes caught sight of something glittering on the ground in front of her. It was a key. Picking it up, Heart saw it was the key to the overcomer's treasure – 'THE MORNING STAR'. She had overcome evil and temptation. She had won over her enemies and won the treasure. She could hardly wait to show her mother. Oh, this really was her favourite key! She hung it carefully with the others, before she ran all the way home.

CHAPTER 7

"A Picnic and a Prisoner'

Heart skipped along the gently winding path leading to Promise Mountain, being careful not to bounce the basket in her hand against her legs. The basket held a picnic lunch of brownie squares, grapes, bananas, crackers and cheese along with several individual boxes of fruit juice.

It really was a picnic-perfect day, and Heart hummed along with the songbirds singing in every tree. She looked up to watch the fluffy white clouds playfully taking turns drifting across the face of the sun, and casting their individually shaped shadows

Heart Longing and the Treasure Keys

on the slopes of Promise Mountain. As she walked, she put words to the tune she had been humming.

*"I'm as carefree as the clouds in a blue, blue, sky
and I love King Vine who is always nigh."*

Heart stopped singing when she reached the foot of Promise Mountain, where she had arranged to meet Star Light, Lily Truthful and Sally Self-Less. They were nowhere in sight. Glancing at her watch, Heart realized she was early. Well, no matter, a few moments to spend on top of Promise Mountain would be an unexpected pleasure.

Heart was soon sitting in her favourite spot, a rock conveniently hollowed out to make a perfect seat. Sitting in it gave her an open view of Eternal Palace. Heart tucked her feet comfortably underneath the rock lip, and rested her chin in her hands. She sighed contentedly. Never, never would she tire of the beauty of the view before her. She watched the Palace shimmering with its glorious light. It was so far away, yet it seemed so very near as well.

Unwillingly, she allowed her eyes to be drawn to the wall surrounding Eternal Palace and to the formidable black door that shut her out. The gray letters over it spelling "DEATH" always made her shudder. Somehow it filled her with dread, and made fear choke her longing to go to that lovely Palace. Determinedly, she pulled her eyes away. Today was too perfect a day to dwell on that door. She would fix her gaze beyond it and just sit and enjoy the golden beauty that lay beyond the glorious

Palace of her King. She felt strangely warm as her thoughts focused on him. She loved him more every day. Never would she have believed she could feel so much love. She smiled. It was because he loved her that she loved him so much in return.

Memories of Mr. Regret and the girl in Mr. Destroyer's house flashed before her eyes, and she felt the familiar ache she always felt when they came to mind. Her face clouded, as thoughts filled her mind. *Why was there an Egypt anyway? Surely with a word and a wave of his hand, King Vine could simply command it to be gone and it would be so! Would Eternal City not be a much better place without the evil presence of Egypt?*

Slowly, she became aware of someone's presence and turning her head, she saw Humble watching with an intense expression on his childlike face. She realized that, somehow, he knew what she was thinking.

"Why Humble?" she asked simply, without explaining her thoughts.

"Why does King Vine allow the evil of Egypt?" Humble repeated her unspoken question. He settled back on his heels beside her and absently picked up a pebble, tossing it up into the air and catching it again as it came down.

"It is a good question, Heart," he finally answered. "Most people don't understand. Maybe I could explain it best by telling you a story."

Heart's eyes sparkled as she leaned forward expectantly. "I love stories," she said with an eager smile.

A gentle smile played at the corners of Humble's mouth. Gazing thoughtfully out at Eternal Palace he began his story.

Heart Longing and the Treasure Keys

"Long, long ago there lived in a vast kingdom, a Prince, who was as good and kind as he was handsome.

It was his pleasure to ride throughout his kingdom surveying all that was his, and to see to the welfare of his subjects. He was rarely recognized in his travels because he took care to keep himself disguised. Announcing his arrival would cause the people to put on false pretenses, and hide away anything unsightly. The Prince wanted to see things as they really were.

One day as the Prince rode through his kingdom, he came upon a beautiful maiden. She was standing in a little meadow, her long golden hair glistening in the sun. The Prince drew nearer. The maiden's long lashes framed eyes as blue as the deepest sea, and her lips were as fresh as morning rose petals. The blush of the rising sun had brushed against her cheeks. In her arms, she held a freshly picked bouquet of delicate meadow flowers. A gentle breeze ruffled the soft folds of her skirt against she legs.

She stood unaware of the Prince's admiring gaze. She did not see him nor the love that was shining in his eyes. How he wanted her for his bride, for her to become his Princess, but wisely, he said nothing. He knew the maiden was young, and her eyes flashed with a carefree zest for life and all its pleasures. Time stretched before her, unblemished and limitless in its promises. The Prince knew if he asked her to be his bride, she would consent and, for a time, would be happy enough as his wife. But then, she would become restless, wondering if perhaps she had missed out on something better than her life in the royal palace. Perhaps she could have had a more exciting life somewhere else, without the responsibilities of being a

Princess. And so the Prince quietly turned his horse in the other direction and rode silently away.

In time, the maiden met a young man who courted her, wooed her and won her heart. He gave her a beautiful ring to wear on her finger. He made many promises to her - but he kept not a one. She began to see him for what he really was. Where she had thought him to be gentle and kind, he was cruel and hard. What she had seen as love in his eyes was unveiled as distain. He wanted her only to be his slave, to wait on him hand and foot, ready to fulfill his every whim, without him ever having to do anything for her. Love was destroyed and her heart was crushed. The maiden lived a life of fear and torment. Time now stretched before her, filled with endless toil and drudgery with no escape. The sparkle was gone from her eyes, and moans, instead of laughter, escaped her lips. Then the day came where he demanded his ring back, and he rode away leaving her destitute.

One morning, as she was working in the heat of the sun trying to grow something to eat, a shadow fell over her. Looking up fearfully, expecting that her false lover had come back to taunt her, she saw instead the beautiful face of the prince smiling down on her. She gazed into his eyes and warmed her cold heart in the love she saw there.

Then, softly he spoke, his voice music in her ears, "Will you come with me and be my love?"

She could not answer; she was afraid to believe it would be true. Truly, the Prince wanted HER? Then hesitantly, she nodded. The Prince stooped down and, with a gentle strength, swept her up and set her before him on his horse, his arm firmly around her waist. She rested her head against his shoulder, her heart bursting with humble gratitude. Now she could truly love him. He was her rescuer, her hero. Forever would hardly be long enough for them to express their love for each other."

Humble ended his story and looked into Heart's face. The emotions his story had aroused; sorrow, joy, anger, love had all been reflected on Heart's attentive face as she listened, and now that the story had ended, she was staring at Humble deep in thought.

Slowly she began to speak, "I think I understand your story. The Prince is the King and I am the maiden." Tears glistened in Heart's eyes as she caught a fresh glimpse of the depth of the King's love for her. She waited for the lump in her throat to dissolve before she continued. "Egypt is there so that everyone can see how kind, and good, and loving King Vine is. It is only when we see how evil and cruel life in Egypt is, and how easily we chose the wrong way, that we can truly appreciate the beauty and goodness of King Vine. We cannot freely be his, until we know from what he has saved us."

Humble looked pleased. "You are a good listener, dear Heart. I couldn't have said it better myself. Now you understand." Then, as was his usual manner, Humble slipped quietly away.

Heart stayed behind, still deep in thought about how King Vine was her Prince. Truly, he had caught her up out of World City and made her a citizen of His kingdom. But what a price it had cost him. To lay down his own life to save her - what love that was! What wonderful, unfathomable love!

Heart was not startled when she heard Word dismount behind her. Somehow she had expected him. She turned to smile her welcome. "I was thinking about King Vine," she announced in greeting.

"I know," answered Word discerningly. "It shows on your face."

Heart's face shone in the light of Word's praise. How different it felt from the pleasure Pride's words had given her.

"Word," she said thoughtfully, "I am so grateful to King Vine for loving me so much that he was willing to pay that terrible price to make me his own."

"Yes," agreed Word, a soberness shadowing his face. "He did suffer much. He suffered because he was not recognized as King. He suffered because he was hated." Word spoke slowly and carefully, and the intensity of his next words puzzled Heart. "All those who love him will also be hated and will be treated even as he was treated."

What WAS Word trying to tell her? Heart wondered at Word's strange tone of voice.

"But there is a reward," Word continued. "Treasure for all who take part in his suffering. He has promised a crown of glory to all who suffer for his name's sake."

To Heart the treasure "CROWN OF GLORY" sounded wonderfully thrilling, but what was the other part of Word's message? The treasure was for those who suffered? What was that about?

"The Presence go with you, dear little Heart." Word looked intently at Heart as though he wished to say more.

With a meaningful backward glance, he rode away without another word.

How strange... thought Heart, looking after the commanding figure sitting so straight and tall on horseback. *Word seemed different today, as though his message was especially important.*

Heart did not have long to muse about Word's disturbing message, for shouting voices interrupted her thoughts.

It was her friends, finally arriving and calling to her that they were ready to go! Cupping her hands to her mouth, Heart shouted back, "I'm coming!" Tucking Word's messages in the back of her mind, she ran sure-footed down the familiar path to join her waiting girlfriends.

When Heart arrived breathless at the bottom of Promise Mountain, Star Light said eagerly, "Okay, where are we going for our picnic. You said it was a surprise, Heart!"

"And so it is," said Heart mysteriously, her eyes dancing.

"Well, lead the way then," demanded Lily Truthful. "Let us waste no more time!"

Heart led the way, refusing to give any hints at all about where they were going. When they came to a certain turn in the path, she became even more mysterious. She stopped and with a little giggle said, "Okay girls, from here on you are not allowed to look. You must close your eyes, and I'll lead you."

"Can't we peek just a little?" coaxed Lily.

Heart laughed. "Nice try, Lily, but I anticipated you being tempted to peek so I brought these along." She pulled three blindfolds out of her pocket.

Amid good-natured protests, groans and girlish giggles, the blindfolds were securely tied in place. Having no other choice, the three blindfolded friends were forced to trust Heart's leading. Now and again, one of them stumbled, but whether it was because of the blindfolds or their giggles was hard to tell. Then, suddenly, Heart stopped. "We're here," she announced. Lily, who stood nearest to Heart, put out her hand.

"Hey" she said, "we're standing beside a big tree!"

"You are right!" agreed Heart. "And we're going straight up the trunk."

"Stop kidding, Heart," scolded Sally. "We know you aren't serious and it's no fun being blindfolded anymore."

The others agreed, but Heart insisted she was not joking. The way to go was, indeed, UP. "See," she said, pulling out the rope ladder – then giggled because, of course, her friends couldn't see. "Here is a ladder. One at a time you can climb it. It's really quite safe, I promise."

The girls considered their options for a moment, then, Sally being perhaps a little more adventuresome than the others or maybe just wanting to prove her bravery, agreed to go first. Heart guided Sally's hands to the first rung of the ladder leading up to the tree fort she and Trouble-Free had built. Soon, Sally reached the fort floor and called down encouragement to the others. It wasn't long before all four friends were seated on the floor of the fort.

"Heart," began Lily firmly. "I've had quite enough. I'm going to take my blindfold off whether you like it or not."

Heart Longing and the Treasure Keys

She waited only a second, and when Heart made no immediate protest, all three quickly pulled the blindfolds from their eyes. Their delighted gasps of astonishment were all Heart had hoped they would be, and for a few minutes everyone talked at once, until they all burst out laughing.

The girls spent a delightful afternoon in the fort. What a perfect place it was to girl-talk and laugh and pretend. And their picnic treats were most delicious. It was a unanimous decision that they had never had a better picnic, and they resolved to come again soon.

Too quickly the time passed, and the girls knew they needed to head for home. Reluctantly, the girls tidied up the fort, leaving no sign that anyone had been there. With many backward glances, they were amazed at how cleverly the fort was hidden to those who did not know it was there.

"Does the fort have a name?" asked Lily.

"Fort of Refuge," answered Heart.

They all agreed it was a very good name. It was a perfect place to feel safe and to enjoy a quiet rest.

They were walking through the field of meadow flowers, when Lily Truthful stopped and exclaimed, with a troubled expression, "Look at that sign. It says "UNDERGROUND FOREST OF PERSECUTION". I've never seen that before, have you?" The others shook their heads, as they all stared at the sign wondering what it meant.

"It's strange we didn't notice the sign when we were coming up," repeated Heart, feeling puzzled about why she had never noticed the sign before ... or ... was it new?

"Well, if you remember, three of us were blindfolded!" said Star Light, and then more seriously added. "I really don't think I'd ever want to go there."

"No, me either," chorused the others as they continued on their way home.

They had not gone far, when Heart stopped again with a cry of dismay. "Oh, no, I forgot Mom's picnic basket at the fort, and she made a special point of reminding me to be sure and bring it back. I'll have to run back and get it. No need for all of us to go back. You go on ahead and I'll catch up."

Heart ran all the way back to the fort, climbed up to retrieve the basket, and then climbed back down being careful to tuck the ladder back out of sight behind the vines. She ran as fast as she could to try to catch up with her friends.

But she never did catch up. She was nearing the sign "UNDERGROUND FOREST OF PERSECUTION", and turned her head to glance with apprehension at the gathering darkness under the trees, which stood not far from the path where the sign was posted.

Suddenly, a dark figure dashed out of the forest and before Heart knew what was happening, a hand was clamped hard over her mouth, and she was dragged into the forest. The forest was so dark, she could not see who her captor was nor could she see where he was taking her. Branches hit at her face and scratched her arms. She struggled to free herself, but her strength was no match for whoever held her firm in his grasp. Roughly, her captor gave her a shake and spoke for the first time. "Tell me you hate King Vine and I will let you go," he snarled.

Heart Longing and the Treasure Keys

Heart gasped and opened her mouth but no sound came out. Deny she loved the King? That was impossible. Her blood was rushing into her head and she could taste the fear rising up in her ... and yet, she also had a sense of knowing she was not alone. She knew the Presence was with her. She tried again to speak, and it was as though the words were given her. "No, never will I say those hateful words. I love King Vine and he loves me."

Her captor growled something she did not understand, and then he gave her a hard push. She stumbled forward to keep from falling, and then heard what sounded like an iron gate slamming shut, and her captor's voice snarled behind her. "There, see if you can escape! Where is your beloved King now when you need him?" His words convinced Heart of the security of her prison; she knew escape was nigh impossible.

Where could she be? It was too dark to see, and Heart was afraid to move, so she sat motionless where she had fallen to her knees. She could neither hear nor see anything, and was afraid to even reach out into the darkness to see if she could touch something. Gradually, however, her eyes became accustomed to the dark, and she could make out that she was in a tunnel of some kind with a large gate closing off the entrance. She ran towards it and shook it as hard as she could. The rattling sound it made only echoed with an eerie sound down through the tunnel. The heavy steel bars of the gate made it clear that there was no hope that the gate could be broken open. She began to shout and call for help, but her words were thrown back in empty hollow echoes. Was she really all alone? She knew her family would miss her that evening, but how would they know where to look for her? How could they possibly find her? Was she left here to perish? Discouraged and afraid, she sat down and burst into sobs.

Finally, when she had no tears left and her throat ached, she drew a deep breath and scolded herself, "Crying is not going to get you out of here. Come now - think!! You will need all your wits about you."

Hearing her own voice was a small comfort, and Heart wiped away her tears with the back of her hand. She WASN'T alone, she reminded herself. The Presence was with her; the King had said he would never leave her.

With the entrance of the tunnel securely locked, Heart was left with only one other direction to go - INTO the tunnel. But did she dare? Was it safe? Where did it lead?

Even as she asked these questions, Heart began to move slowly into the tunnel. She was careful to test the ground ahead of her with her foot before she took a step, making sure it safe with no sudden drop offs.

It seemed forever that she had been walking, and her body was aching from the stiff, careful way she was forced to walk. She was tempted to go back, knowing at least the tunnel was safe this far in. She took one more step, thinking it would be her last before she turned around, but then the tunnel took a sharp turn to the left, and Heart's body began to tremble. She was sure she could just make out a tiny beam of light at what would seem to be the end of the tunnel. At the same moment, her left hand guiding her along the side of the tunnel suddenly felt nothing, nothing except empty space. The wall had ended. Heart stared into the blackness willing her eyes to see. She could just make out that there was a fork in the tunnel. Heart did not consider long which way to go. The light at the end of the right fork drew her, and slowly, carefully, she made her way toward it. Yes, now she was sure. The light was getting brighter and Heart moved faster. Soon she would make her escape out of the tunnel. *But,* she thought, *would she know where she was? Or would she encounter a new challenge?*

CHAPTER 8

"Rescued"

Heart had reached the end of the tunnel, and now she saw that the light she had been walking toward shone down from above her. Looking up, she could see a spot of blue sky. Freedom was within her reach. Hope surged within her. Hanging against the stone wall, was a ladder just waiting for her to climb up out of the dark terrifying tunnel. Heart did not question how the ladder had come to be so conveniently hung there. She was simply thankful that it was.

With some trepidation, excitement and fearful hope, Heart grasped hold of the first rung, and with a deep trembling breath began to climb. She finally reached the last rung and swung one leg over the top. With a final effort, she pulled herself away from the tunnel shaft and stood to her feet.

A cry of dismay caught in her throat. She had not stepped into freedom at all!

Instead, she saw with mounting dread that she was standing in the centre of Egypt! Standing before her, sturdy legs astride, and a sinister grin of self-satisfaction on his face, was her captor.

"I knew I could expect you," he said with a snort. "Saved me dragging you out here, how considerate of you to come all on your own." He laughed, but the expression on his face made Heart wish she was far away. She thought about making a dash for it and looked around furtively, but her captor, sensing her intentions, grabbed her roughly by one arm. Amid the jeers of the gathering crowd, he hurried her off, stumbling as she went, until they came to a cement building surrounded by a high fence topped with lights and barbed wire. A big guard standing in front of the heavy steel door let them in, coldly chuckling as he commented, "Another one, huh?"

Her captor mumbled a reply, but Heart did not understand what he said. Still holding her by one arm, almost wrenching her shoulder out of place, he dragged her down a narrow damp corridor until he stopped and pushing open a creaking, rusted door, shoved her none too gently, into a cold dismal space. He locked the door behind him and left, his cruel laughter echoing eerily in the empty corridor gradually fading away as his footsteps faded farther and farther away. *Oh not again*, thought Heart. *Am I really a prisoner again?*

Heart looked around her. It was not completely dark - a little light came in through a roughly hewn hole high in the outside wall. The hole was securely covered by a dirty grate, but it would have been too small for her to crawl though even if she could have reached it. The door from the corridor also had a small window in it and was set in a solid wall. The walls to her left and right were like bars of cages, through which she could make out other cells similar to the one she was in.

Her cell was empty, except for a metal frame that was supposedly meant to serve as a bed. An old board was laid on top for a mattress. There was no blanket, and the room felt chillingly damp. An odd odour permeated the room, musty and pungent. Heart could hardly breathe for the stench.

Weary, frightened, and confused, Heart walked over to the bed, sat down on the rough board, and dropping her face into her hands, began to weep.

After a time her sobs became less violent, and she stopped shaking. She lifted her head. Strangely, even though she was more frightened than she had ever been in her whole life, she still had that comforting feeling deep inside that she was not alone. Could it be that King Vine had not deserted her after all? Could he, even here, still be with her? But why had he allowed her to be taken to this awful place? From a picnic in the Fort of Refuge to a cell? How very long ago that picnic seemed. Had Lily, Sally and Star Light told her parents that something had happened to her? Or had they simply decided that she must have gone home by another path. Maybe no-one would become alarmed until late tonight. And when her parents did realize that something was wrong, they would never think of looking for her in Egypt. Maybe she would have to stay here the rest of her life. The thought made Heart start to cry all over again. Would she never see her family again? But then, stronger than before, she felt the Presence of the King comfort her.

Heart, feeling totally exhausted, tried to lie down and sleep but she was so cold and uncomfortable that sleep was impossible.

Oh, King Vine, she thought, *I am so cold!*

Sensing, rather than hearing anything, she looked up to see a soft figure of light move toward her. She felt no fear. Then, something comfortingly warm enfolded her, and she murmured softly to herself, "One of the King's messengers from Eternal Palace." She slept.

She did not know how long she had been asleep, but suddenly, something startled her awake. Opening her eyes, she could see it was morning by the light that came in through the tiny window, but that was not what had awakened her. Heart sat up, listening. There! There it was again. This time, she recognized the sound; it was a key turning in a lock. Someone was at her cell door. But no, she was mistaken. It was not her door, but the door to the cell beside her. Heart watched as the door opened, and to her dismay, Lily and Sally were pushed into the room and the door banged shut behind them.

The three girls stared at one another, not sure whether to laugh or cry at being together again.

"Where is Star Light?" asked Heart anxiously.

"She got away. They didn't catch her," said Lily.

"Do you have any idea why we are here?" asked Heart hopefully.

"Well," answered Sally, "we heard a little of what people were saying at the place we were kept for the night. It seems Mr. Destroyer hates anyone who loves King Vine, and he wants to stop people from being his followers. He wants to make everyone live in Egypt. We angered him when we spurned his invitation to enjoy his city and he is determined to make us pay."

"But he can't make us live there!" protested Heart.

"No?" asked Lily quietly. "Then why don't we just go home?"

The girls looked at the bars and the locked doors and realized that, willing or not, they were the prisoners of Mr. Destroyer.

"At least I wouldn't deny King Vine when they tried to make me," said Heart firmly.

"No," agreed Lily and Sally, "neither did we."

The friends smiled at each other. Mr. Destroyer could hold them prisoners, but he could not take them away from King Vine.

Heart asked the question that all of them were thinking, but too afraid to say out loud, "What do you think they are going to do with us?"

"I don't know," answered Lily, "but I do know that they will do all they can to persuade us to stop loving King Vine."

Heart Longing and the Treasure Keys

"Well, they can't do that," insisted Heart. "Maybe they can keep me in this cell, but they can't change what I know is true!"

"You are right!" agreed the other girls. "And surely King Vine will help us!"

"He already has," said Heart softly, and she told them how a messenger from Eternal Palace had brought warmth and comfort to her in the night. It made all of them feel better to know that the King was not far away and that he knew what was happening to them. For a time they sat in silence, each in her own thoughts. They were cold, miserable, and hungry, but still they were filled with peace. They lost track of how many hours they sat on the cold floor, but they could no longer find a comfortable position that would not cramp their limbs or put them to sleep.

Their attention was drawn to approaching footsteps and then the sound of a key. This time it WAS Heart's door. She stared as the door opened, but it was not her captor who stood there as she had supposed. Instead, to her surprise, it was the unhappy looking girl she had seen at Mr. Destroyer's house. Her long, tangled brown hair looked like it had not been brushed in a long time. A brown sack dress that hung shapeless from her shoulders was stained and rumpled as though she had slept in it.

"I've brought your food," she stated tonelessly, and set a bowl of soup on the floor in front of Heart. It didn't smell very good, but Heart realized she was hungry enough to eat most anything. Maybe it would taste better than it smelled. When she saw the girl had brought no spoon, she raised the bowl to her mouth. She took a little sip but quickly spat it out.

"Bah!" she said. "That's awful!"

"Fine," responded the girl unsympathetically. "You don't have to eat. I don't care if you starve. Anyway, I'm supposed to bring you to Mr. Destroyer. He wants to see you."

She held the door open for Heart to go through and then, as if reading the hope in Heart's eyes, warned. "It's no use trying to escape. They'll catch you quicker than you could take five steps. If you know what's good for you, just follow me."

She stepped out into the darkened corridor. Heart looked back for encouragement from her friends, and then followed the girl.

It wasn't far to Mr. Destroyers' house. Heart remembered it well from the first time she had been there.

Mr. Destroyer was waiting for her in the garish front room. "Well, well, how nice to see you again, Heart. Have you and Molly Miserable become friends?" *So that's her name*, thought Heart. She glanced at Molly, but Molly did not meet her eyes and did not speak a word.

"Really," scolded Mr. Destroyer in mock severity. "You must learn to be more friendly, Molly. Well, never mind! Go help your mother in the kitchen."

When she had gone, Mr. Destroyer turned to Heart.

"You must be hungry and tired. I heard what happened to you. Such a shame. Here, come and sit down." He led her to the adjoining room, and pointed to a table laden with all of Heart's favourite food. It smelled so good! Tempting that it was, and though her mouth watered, Heart was determined that she would not eat anything in Mr. Destroyer's home. Mr. Destroyer

Heart Longing and the Treasure Keys

rose and came over to the table sitting down opposite her and began to eat. He did not encourage Heart to fill her plate too, in fact, he did not say anything about the food at all.

"I was quite disturbed to hear you had been brought against your will to Egypt. I am so sorry for the way you have been treated. I want to make it up to you, and I tell you it really was not by my orders that you were captured."

Heart stared at Mr. Destroyer. He looked and sounded so sincere. Could it be that this had all just been a terrible mistake? She tried to moisten her mouth; she was so thirsty. Maybe just a sip of the glass of water at her plate would be OK. She took one sip and felt the cool water trickle down her throat. It felt so good! Without thinking about what she was doing, she began to eat of the delicious food before her. It was very good, and she was so hungry.

Half beginning to trust Mr. Destroyer, she thought of her friends still in that horrible dungeon.

"What about Lily and Sally, my friends?" she asked.

"How thoughtful of you. I admire how you are so quick to think of others. Don't worry; they have everything I'm offering you."

No longer suspecting any evil intent on Mr. Destroyer's part, Heart relaxed, and enjoyed the meal set before her.

When Heart had eaten all she could, she sat back and said, "Thank you, Mr. Destroyer. That was most delicious."

"Much better than what you'd get in that cell you were in," said Mr. Destroyer slyly. "I really would like to make up for the horrible night you must have spent there. I see that you collect treasure keys. Yours are very beautiful, but I understand the treasure itself is not yours yet."

"Oh yes!" corrected Heart quickly. "It is mine. King Vine is keeping it for me in his Palace."

"But you can't HAVE it right now, can you?" probed Mr. Destroyer cunningly. He pulled out a huge golden key out of his pocket and held it out Heart. "This key unlocks any treasure found in Egypt. With this key, there is nothing in Egypt you cannot have and enjoy right now."

"No thank you," refused Heart, suddenly suspicious. "I don't want it."

Mr. Destroyer stretched his lips open sideways but it hardly resembled a smile. He leaned forward, his voice becoming strangely hypnotic. "You don't understand. Egypt would be yours. You could eat a banquet like you just enjoyed any time you wished. Anything that caught your fancy could be yours for the taking. This key unlocks all the treasures of Egypt. Everything you see would by yours." He paused, and then added meaningfully, "You don't, of course, even have to live here. Just come to visit whenever you want."

As Mr. Destroyer talked, he waved the key in front of Heart's face, and as she stared at it, it seemed to become bigger and bigger. She blinked and then rubbed her eyes. Why was she getting so sleepy, and why was it so hard to think, and why did Mr. Destroyer's voice sound so funny. The key WAS nice. There WERE many things she wanted, and the thought of how she could share her bounty with others added to the temptation. All she needed was that key. The food, the

Heart Longing and the Treasure Keys

treasures, the servants, the power, oh yes, she wanted the key, it was a g o o d k e y. Why did she feel so funny? Why did her words sound themselves out letter by letter? It was so h a r d to think clearly … O h, y e s … the key … it wa s all about the .. the …. Heart tried hard to focus her eyes on the key, and she lifted her hand to reach for it when something startled her and she drew back her hand. There was Conscience sitting on the back of a chair flapping his wings to get her attention. She blinked at him … W h y … why… was it so h a r d to keep her eyes open?

"Remember Word's message, 'Beware of the treasure of Egypt'," he said and off he flew, gliding out through an open window. It was enough to make Heart shake herself awake. She struggled to keep her eyes open and willed the fog out of her mind.

"No, Mr. Destroyer," she said, forcing the words out slowly and clearly. "I do not want your key, and I really must be going home. My parents will be worried."

Mr. Destroyer suddenly changed before her eyes. He dropped all pretence of being kind or friendly. His cruel and ugly face grew red with rage.

"Joe Captor!" he shouted. "Take Heart back to her cell. She likes it there!"

By the time she was delivered back into her cell, her mind felt clear again and the drowsiness had passed. She explained what had happened and Lily and Sally agreed that the water and the food must have been drugged. All three made up their minds to stay on guard, never, never to eat any food offered them by Mr. Destroyer. He was a liar. Nothing he said could be believed to be true.

No-one came near them for the rest of the day, and they spent a cold lonely night in their cells.

Early the next morning, Joe Captor came again. In his hand, he carried three lengths of rope. Without explanation, he tied the hands of each girl behind her back, then roughly prodded them forward into the prison corridor.

"Go!" he commanded and whistled a whip through the air in warning.

A chilling fear swept over Heart and her friends. He wasn't going to whip them, was he?

Taking them outside the prison, he made them walk up and down the streets lined with people who laughed and taunted, mocked and sneered at the spectacle the three prisoners made. Some threw tomatoes and eggs at them, some even threw rocks. But although all three were splattered with egg yolks and tomato juice, not one rock hit them. Once Heart looked up to see a rock hurling straight toward her head. She was just about to duck when it was as though an invisible hand blocked the rock, and it fell harmlessly at her feet.

The girls felt they had been made to stumble up and down the streets for hours. Their wrists were raw where the ropes were rubbing, and their backs and shoulders ached from being forced to walk in an awkward position.

The crowd in front of them suddenly parted, revealing a large wire cage set up in the middle of the street. Their captor pushed them inside and snapped the lock on the cage door.

The people surged closer around them shouting, "Deny the King, Deny the King!" It seemed to Heart and her friends that the cruel voices were far away and really not directed at them at all, and they hardly took notice of the objects being thrown at the cage. All they were aware of was the very real Presence that encircled them.

"Let's sing," suggested Lily softly, and she began to sing a praise song to the King. Heart and Sally joined in. At first they sang too softly for anyone to hear them, but then courage began to rise up within them, and raising their voices, they sang in beautiful harmony. King Vine WAS worthy to be praised, no matter where they were, and as they sang, joy began to fill them.

One by one the people stopped their shouting and moved slowly away until only Joe Captor was left. He scowled at the girls and threatened them if they did not stop their singing. But they only sang the louder. They were so full of the love of the King that there was no room for fear.

"Just wait until tomorrow," Joe Captor snarled, in the voice that was now familiar to the girls. "If you thought today was hard, wait until tomorrow. Mr. Destroyer has ways of dealing with those who refuse his golden key to Egypt's treasure. You have made him very angry. He is, even now, planning his revenge." With that, Joe Captor also left, leaving the girls alone in the middle of a deserted street. Well, not quite deserted. There was one who had not left when the girls had started stinging, and now she came out from behind the billboard where she had hidden to watch. It was Molly Miserable. She walked slowly toward the cage. As the girls watched her approach,

Heart felt a flood of emotion toward her. The poor girl. Heart had never seen anyone look so miserable. Molly did not speak until she stood right in front of the cage.

"Why did you sing?" she asked abruptly. "I never heard anyone sing like that before."

"We sang because we know the King of Eternal City. He is with us, and will not desert us. He will help us. Because we love and trust him, we like to sing our praises to him," explained Heart.

"But don't you hate being like an animal in a cage with no food, and people throwing things at you, and calling you horrible names?" asked Molly.

"We hardly noticed," answered Heart thoughtfully.

"You are very strange," decided Molly. "Why won't you do what Mr. Destroyer says? Maybe then we could be friends.

"I don't have any friends," she added, rather wistfully.

"We cannot do what Mr. Destroyer wants," replied Heart patiently. "We must obey the King, but you CAN be our friend. You can enter Eternal City and belong to King Vine too."

"But I don't want to leave Egypt," protested Molly. "I like it here. I've never lived anywhere else. I'm sorry you won't obey Mr. Destroyer. I have to go now, before he misses me. Good bye!"

She darted quickly down the now empty street toward the Destroyer house. The three friends watched until Molly turned a corner and then listened as the echo of her footsteps faded away.

They were alone in a street that was rarely deserted. What were they going to do? But even as they asked the question,

Heart Longing and the Treasure Keys

they laughed ruefully. Locked in the cage, there was not much they COULD do except wait. Night was fast approaching and with it came some relief from the heat. It never became really dark even in the side streets of Egypt, the city's night lights were strange, eerie lights that cast hideous shadows beyond their reach.

The cage was too small for the girls to lie down, so they tried to settle themselves as comfortable as possible, leaning against one another as they sat with their knees drawn up to their chests. The thick wire on the bottom and sides of the cage bit into their legs and their shoulders. They shifted their weight into new positions, easing the cramping of one limb, but quickly finding it simply transferred the pain to another. The end result didn't change, pain and discomfort was their lot in the cage. If only Joe Captor would have loosened the rope around their wrists, but that would have been too kind.

Though at first the cooler temperatures were a relief, it wasn't long before the chilly breezes sent shivers along the arms and legs of the three hungry prisoners confined in an animal cage. Had it not been for the Presence still around them, they would have been most miserable.

In spite of their agony, the girls were so tired they drifted into a dreamless sleep. How long they slept they had no idea, but Sally's sudden sharp intake of breath startled them awake.

"What is it, Sally?" they whispered, their eyes searching the dark shadows that surrounded them.

"There, over there, something is moving," whispered Sally, hoarsely, pointing with her nose.

Heart and Lily looked carefully, willing their eyes to adjust to the dim light. Yes, there it was … they saw it too. A black shadowy form was moving stealthily from building to building, obviously taking great care to stay within the darkest shadows. Whoever it was, did not want to be seen.

The girls watched, hardly breathing. They did not know, did not dare to guess, but was it friend? or was it foe?

The figure drew closer and the girls could make out the fluttering of a black cape, but it was hooded, so they were prevented from seeing the man's face - if indeed it was a man. He was, now, just on the other side of the street. He hesitated for a moment, and then made one last limping, dash across the street and slid into a crouched position beside the girl's cage. He leaned against it as though he was exhausted. The girls heard his heavy breathing, but he said nothing. The girls were too frightened to make a sound.

"Don't cry out," he finally cautioned unnecessarily. "I come as a friend."

The girls let out their breath simultaneously in a whooshing sound of relief. Then Sally exclaimed in a stage whisper, "Why, it's Mr. Regret! He's come to help us. Oh, how thankful we are to you!" She directed the last part of her remark to the black caped figure but he did not answer.

He began to fumble with the cage's lock.

"Oh, King Vine," breathed Heart, "you sent Mr. Regret to help us. Now, please help him to open the lock."

For a few long moments, it looked as though Mr. Regret could not manage the mechanics of the lock, then, quite

Heart Longing and the Treasure Keys

suddenly it fell open in his hands. He wasted no time cutting them free from the ropes that tied them.

"There!" he said in a satisfied tone. "There! You are free to go. Stay close to the buildings so no one will see you and follow the 'Way Provided' home."

"But, aren't you coming with us?" protested Sally.

"No, no," replied Mr. Regret sadly, "It's too late for me, too late for me. I should have gone long ago. It's too late now. Go quickly, go quickly while there is still time for you." Pulling his cloak around him, he turned and quickly faded into the shadows before the girls could stop him.

The friends momentarily forgot they were free, staring with concern and disappointment into the shadows where they had last seen Mr. Regret. Lily came to herself first and grabbed Heart and Sally's hands, exclaiming, "Hurry, what we are waiting for? LET'S GO!"

The "WAY PROVIDED" was still as hidden as before, but the three girls had no trouble finding it and ran as fast as they could until they reached the Stream of Refreshing. They threw themselves on the bank to rest and drink of the sweet water.

They didn't rest for long, just long enough to rub some of the stiffness from their arms and legs. Then, they continued on their way, so anxious to get home.

Before the sun rose the next morning, all three girls were safely back home. What a joyful reunion there was in three Eternal City homes that morning. The girls told their stories over and over again as the neighbours and friends, all having heard the good news, stopped by, eager to see for themselves.

Everyone admired their new keys – keys to the treasure of "THE CROWN OF LIFE". They had refused to deny their King, choosing rather to suffer the consequences, even if their lives were threatened. Their reward was more treasure laid up for them in Eternal Palace.

CHAPTER 9

"Mother Robin's Lesson"

Everywhere Heart, Sally, and Lily went, people reached out to clasp their hands or clap a hand on their shoulders, to express their joy that they were safely home again. Over and over, the girls were asked questions about the details of their adventure. They had become celebrities.

Heart and her two friends had received an invitation to go to the Annual Picnic Fair as the year's honoured guests. It was, without a doubt, a most exciting thing to happen to them. They looked forward to the fair with eager anticipation. The Annual Fair was a highly anticipated and well attended event. More activities and displays were added each year, and it climaxed with a spectacular explosion of fireworks.

Finally, the awaited day arrived! It dawned clear and sunny, promising to be a perfect day!

Heart awakened early and bounded out of bed. She was determined to savor every minute of this special day. Her friends would soon be at her door, and then they would be off to enjoy the fair.

As soon as Heart skipped into the kitchen she stopped, instantly sensing something was wrong. The kitchen was strangely quiet and empty. Where was her mother?

"Heart, is that you? Are you up?" Heart barely recognized her mother's voice calling from the bedroom; it was weak and hoarse sounding.

"What's wrong, Mom?" she asked, stepping to the bedroom door. One look at her mother and her eyes filled with tears. Not today! Oh please not today! Her mother just COULDN'T be sick today!

"Oh, Mom, you aren't sick, are you?" she asked, even though she already knew the answer. Her day was about to be spoiled; she just knew it.

"I'm so sorry, Heart. I wouldn't have spoiled this your day for anything, but I'm afraid I'm just too sick to get out of bed."

"Well ...," Heart's mind was racing, desperate to find a way to save the day, "isn't there someone who could come stay with you?"

Heart Longing and the Treasure Keys

Just then, Miss Favor came walking into her mother's room and heard Heart's last remark. "I don't want anyone to come stay," she whined in a funny weepy voice.

"Come here, Miss Favor," said her mother gently, and touched her forehead. "Oh, no, you are feverish too. I'm sorry, Heart, but everyone else will want to go to the fair. I'm afraid we just won't be able to manage without your help today."

Heart turned away and went back into the kitchen so her mother would not see the tears that ran unchecked down her cheeks. Miss Favor's pitiful whimpering and her mother's soothing voice followed her. It just wasn't fair! She had so looked forward to today. And now, she wouldn't be an honoured guest at the fair with her friends, and she would be missing in the front page photos that would surely be taken for tomorrow's newspaper. Her disappointment cut deep.

She was still standing in the kitchen when a happy rat-a-tat-tat knock sounded at the door. With a heavy heart, knowing it was her friends, she slowly went to the door and opened it.

The grin on Sally's face faded as soon as she looked at Heart. "Whatever is wrong?" she asked anxiously. "You CAN'T be sick!"

"No," answered Heart in a self-pitying voice, "but everyone else is. I have to play nursemaid!"

"Oh, no!" sympathized Sally. "You just can't! Today is OUR day! We're the honoured guests and all. They will be taking our pictures and want us to tell our story and everything. You just CAN'T not be there!"

Heart was trying hard not to let the huge lump in her throat trigger a new flood of tears.

Sally reached out to touch Heart's arm. "Listen, is there something I can do? Do you want me to stay with you?" she added impulsively.

Heart smiled gratefully through tear filled eyes. "You are the best kind of friend, Sally, but it would be silly for both of us to miss the fair. No, you and Lily go and have a wonderful time. It will make me feel better to know that my friends are having a super day." Heart's voice shook a little, but she managed to keep the tears back.

"Okay," agreed Sally reluctantly, yet, somehow relieved too. "I guess you are right."

She turned to go, then she looked back at Heart and said gently, "I don't know how to make you feel better, but I know King Vine will, somehow, help you. We'll sure miss you!"

Heart watched Sally until she was out of sight, then she slowly closed the door, feeling miserable.

With a downcast look and dragging feet, Heart went back into the bedroom.

"Would you like something to drink or eat, Mom?" she asked woodenly.

"A drink would be nice, Heart, thank you. I am really sorry that you have to miss the fair."

"Me too, me too, I want a drink too," insisted Miss Favor, resting her hot little head on her mother's shoulder.

"Yes, little Sis," sighed Heart. "I'll bring you a drink too."

Heart Longing and the Treasure Keys

Back in the kitchen, Heart mixed some packaged powdered orange juice with tap water, poured it into two glasses, and with one glass in each hand, turned to take them to the bedroom.

Loud twitters caught her attention, and she looked out the window to see what the fuss was about. There on the grass was a red-breasted robin, cheerfully cocking her head first to one side, then to the other.

She's listening for her breakfast, thought Heart. She watched the robin hop ... hop again ... and then hop the other way, looking as cheerful as only a happy robin could look. Heart felt her self-pity sink even deeper as she considered that even the birds got to do what they wanted.

There, Heart smiled in spite of herself. *She got her breakfast - a nice big, juicy, fat, long worm.*

As she watched, she realized where the loud twitters had come from. Two almost fully grown young robins came hopping up when they saw breakfast hanging from their mother's beak.

That's not fair, frowned Heart, looking at the young robins, *you are plenty big enough to get your own worms. That is your mother's worm. She had such fun catching it, let her enjoy it!*

But to Heart's surprise, Mother Robin took a flying hop to meet one of her young and put the worm in his mouth. The other robin protested loudly, demanding he be fed as well.

Mother Robin took no offense, and repeated her listening-hopping-listening dance until she pulled another fat worm for her other big baby.

Heart did not move as she watched Mother Robin continue to feed first one, then the other, never seeming to give a thought to eating one herself. Yet, as much as the young robins ate and demanded more, Mother Robin never lost that happy cheerful way about her. She seemed to love what she was doing, as if there was nothing she would rather do.

The lesson played out for her in the yard, sank deep into Heart's mind. She realized it was meant for her to watch, and she felt ashamed when she compared herself to Mother Robin.

If Mother Robin could be so happy finding worms to feed her hungry, greedy brood, could she not be happy caring for the family she loved? What was it Word said yesterday, "Whatever you do, do it for the King and from him you will receive your rewards." She thought he meant for her to be there for the people at the fair, but maybe he had meant something else.

Alright then, she would spend today serving the King. There would always be another fair next year, even if she wouldn't be an honoured guest.

"Thank you, Mother Robin," said Heart softly. "You are very wise. Thank you for teaching me something today."

As if she understood, Mother Robin looked up to Heart's face in the open window and sang a pretty trill before she flew away, her babies following her with loud protests.

Heart turned away from the window and looked at the two glasses of lukewarm juice in her hands. No, no, this wouldn't do at all. It was NOT good enough for the King.

Humming a happy little tune, with her eyes sparking with pleasure, Heart was soon as cheerful as Mother Robin as she bustled about in the kitchen.

Heart Longing and the Treasure Keys

Remembering what her mother had done for her the last time she'd had a fever, she went into her mother's bedroom with a cool cloth to wash Miss Favor's flushed little face and hands. She laid another cloth across her mother's forehead.

"Thank you, dear Heart," she said gratefully. "I wanted to get one for myself, but I'm just too dizzy to get up. That feels so good!"

Miss Favor even giggled a little as Heart traced the letter "F" on her cheek with the corner of the washcloth.

Then, she fluffed the pillows for her mother and Miss Favor and assured them that breakfast would be served shortly.

The tray that Heart brought to the bed was so pretty that her Mom caught her breath. "Why Heart," she exclaimed, "that is the prettiest tray I have ever seen! Just looking at it makes me feel better, and the little vase of sweet peas is so pretty."

"Can I smell the flowers?" asked Miss Favor, momentarily forgetting her throbbing head.

After breakfast, Heart took the tray back to the kitchen and washed the dishes she had used. Then, she suggested, "Why don't I take Miss Favor back to her own bed, so you can get some rest, Mom."

"Good idea, thank you," sighed her mother. Heart looked at her mother anxiously. It was so unlike her mother to stay in bed. She really must feel awful. "Oh, Heart, would you mind watering my plants? I forgot yesterday, and I don't want them to wilt."

"Sure, Mom," answered Heart cheerfully.

Picking up Miss Favor, Heart carried her to her own room, promising to tell her stories about King Vine. Tucking her into her bed, she sat down beside her and told her story after story about how much King Vine loved her and how good he was. Miss Favor listened with a thoughtful expression and then had a question. "Heart, if I have two stuffed bunnies would the King be pleased if I gave one to my friend who doesn't have any?"

Heart smiled, "I think he would be very pleased if you did that."

Miss Favor finally fell asleep. Still smiling, Heart gently covered her little sister with a light blanket and tip toed from the room.

Filling a pitcher with water, Heart began to water her mother's flower pots. Again, Word's message came to her mind, "Everything you do, do as unto the King."

Even water plants? thought Heart. Then the thought occurred to her, *well, what if these were the King's plants, how would I water them then?*

It was as though her eyes had been opened. She noticed the rims of some of some of the pots were dusty, some of the leaves had turned brown, and some of the blooms needed deadheading.

Now, instead of a quick watering, each plant received careful attention. When she was finished, Heart wished the King could see them; they looked so nice. Then she smiled, well perhaps he could see them; yes, she was sure he could.

All day, nothing was too much trouble for Heart. Each request, each demand, was met with a willing smile. Miss Favor even decided it was fun to be sick if Heart took care of her and announced that she was going to be sick more often. Heart laughed and remarked, "I think you must be feeling better!"

With the help of her mother's instructions, Heart had supper ready when her father and brother came home.

"How is your mother?" was her father's first question, when he walked in the door. "I would have stayed home if I could have given my job responsibilities to someone else, but everyone that could have filled in for me was going to the fair."

"I really think she is feeling better," answered Heart. "She drank a lot, and I heated some soup for lunch, and she slept some too."

"Good," was her father's relieved reply. "Sounds like you've been a good little nurse maid!" Her father's praise warmed Heart from the inside out.

Later, when supper had been cleared away and Miss Favor was asleep for the night, Heart slipped outside and sat down on a stump in the front yard. It was then that she realized how tired she was. She'd been running all day, trying to keep her patients comfortable and happy. Miss Favor had quite enjoyed having someone so eager to come and go at her beck and call, and she had kept Heart busy.

"But the funny thing," thought Heart out loud, "is that it really WAS fun!"

There was a feeling of contentment that wrapped Heart like a blanket.

A flash of colour in the distance caught Heart's attention as she heard the sounds of fireworks exploding against the night sky.

"Oh," she exclaimed with delight, realizing that she was not going to miss the fireworks after all.

She did not hear the approaching footsteps, nor did she see anyone coming up the path until she was aware of someone standing directly behind her and a hand on her shoulder. She sprang to her feet and then gasped when she realized who had joined her. It was none other than King Vine.

"Oh, King Vine!" whispered Heart, almost speechless with wonder at his beauty.

King Vine smiled, his love shining on his face. "Heart," he said in his rich voice, "you have served me all day long." Smiling again at Heart's look of amazement, he continued. "Yes, I was watching you care for your family. I saw your cheerful attitude, I felt the love you showed. And I saw you telling Miss Favor about me and teaching her to know and love me. And you never had one thought about gaining something for yourself. You found your joy in serving others. You found much treasure today, dear Heart. Look, I have brought you your new keys." And he held out to Heart two shiny gold keys.

Long after King Vine had gone, Heart still felt the warmth of his love. She sat, the fireworks forgotten, admiring the lovely new keys that lay in her hand.

She was still there when Lily and Sally walked by on their way home.

"Heart," they called, when they spied her still sitting outside, bathed in the light of the full moon.

"Sally, Lily!" responded Heart running toward them. "How was the fair?"

"Oh, it was such fun!" Lily and Sally answered enthusiastically. "But the fireworks were the best."

"I could see most of them from here, and they were amazing!" agreed Heart.

"Is that a new treasure key in your hand?" asked Lily, suddenly noticing something shining in Heart's hand.

"Yes, it is," replied Heart with a smile, holding up her special keys. "Two of them!"

"But how did you get them? Weren't you home all day?" questioned Lily, a puzzled frown creasing her forehead.

"Yes," answered Heart, "but I learned something wonderful today. We can find treasure anywhere if we remember Word's message to do whatever we do as if we were doing it for King Vine.

Lily and Sally were silent for moment, reflecting on what Heart had said. Then, Sally broke the silence asking, "Have you found your keys on your treasure map?"

"No, I haven't had a chance yet. But why don't we look now? I have my map right here."

Heart pulled her map out of her pocket and spread it out under the light of the full moon. Three heads bent over the map.

"Here it is!" exclaimed Sally, being the first to find it. And there were the markers – not far from each other were the signs for the "CROWN OF GLORY" treasure and the "DOING UNTO HIM" treasure.

"We could so easily have missed them," mused Lily. "I really think you had as much fun today as we did, Heart Longing. Maybe even more!"

"I think I did too," Heart smiled happily at her friends as they made plans for the next day.

Heart's last thought, as her head nestled into her pillow that night, was that doing everything for King Vine turned every task into a joyous one, and to have his praise was more important that having anyone else's.

Mrs. Longing tip-toed into Heart's bedroom a few minutes later, and stood looking down at her daughter - sound asleep with a smile on her peaceful face.

She has been like an angel today, thought Mrs. Longing-Fulfilled. *I know how much she wanted to go to the fair, yet she never grumbled all day. In fact, she acted as though she'd have chosen to be home instead of at the fair. She's a treasure of a daughter to me.* She bent and kissed Heart gently on her forehead, then tip-toed back out of the room, closing the door softly behind her.

CHAPTER 10

"A Prized Possession"

Heart ran up the path leading to the top of Promise Mountain. It seemed too long since she'd been there, and this morning the desire was especially strong. The path was now so familiar to Heart that her steps were sure and nimble, until she reached the rock she loved to rest on.

The sun was just rising, its early morning light-beams brushing the sky with deep pink strokes. The sunrise cast the most beautiful glow over Eternal Palace, and Heart never tired of looking at it.

Someday, she thought dreamily, *someday I'm going to live there with King Vine. How exciting that will be! Oh, sometimes I just cannot wait!*

But then, as always when she thought of going to Eternal Palace, her eyes turned to that awful, black door in the wall. Why did she have to go through that door marked DEATH. It looked SO frightening.

Hearing footsteps coming nearer, Heart looked around in surprise. It wasn't often someone else came to the top of Promise Mountain.

A young man had climbed up to a spot not far from where Heart was sitting. He did not notice her, and Heart watched him with interest as he stood staring at Eternal Palace.

She watched as Word rode up on his magnificent horse and drew up beside the young man. Dismounting, he turned to him and began to converse with him.

"Beautiful, so beautiful," the young man murmured. "Someday, someday I would like to go there."

He turned to Word, "Tell me," he asked earnestly, "what must I do to have a place reserved for me in Eternal Palace?"

"You are a good man," observed Word thoughtfully. "You always try to do that which is right. You are honest in business and treat your employees fairly. You work hard to provide for your family, pay your taxes, and give your pocket change to the beggars on the street corner."

"Yes," agreed the young man nodding eagerly. "From the time I was old enough to understand right from wrong I have always done everything I knew was right to do."

"You have done well," agreed Word, "but it is not enough to reserve a place for you in Eternal Palace"

The young man was astonished and asked, "Then pray tell me what else I must do and I will do it!"

"To reserve a place for yourself in Eternal Palace," answered Word carefully, with a searching glance at the young man who was hanging on his every word, "you must love the King with your WHOLE heart – that is, more than you love yourself. You have been blessed in the work of your hands and have gathered in abundance the gold and silver of this world. You have bought for yourself houses, cars, and everything that caught your fancy. You have indulged your every whim and given to others grudgingly, and then only what you didn't want for yourself. Your motive for doing right was so others would think highly of you. You must be willing to give of your best - sell what you do not need and give it to those who are poor."

The young man drew back with a startled look at Word. "But," he protested with a scowl, "I have worked hard for the things I have. Why should I give to those who have not worked as hard as I have? Why should they deserve to be blessed by MY labour?"

Word spoke gently to the young man, "If you put the King first in your life and the need of others before your own, you will have treasure in Eternal Palace and the promise that one day, you too, will live there." Word sorrowfully studied the young man who was biting his lower lip, his struggling emotions imprinted on his face.

Heart did not realize she was holding her breath as she watched the young man. Oh, surely, surely he would agree to share with others his great blessings. Was Eternal treasure not worth so much more than any of his earthly possessions? Heart listened in disbelief to the young man's final words. "You must be mistaken. It can't cost all that. I am willing to do anything to enter Eternal Palace, but I cannot give up the things I have earned, the things that I love."

He turned, his sadness evident on his face. He walked down the mountain, his steps quickening as he went.

Heart felt sorrow wash over her, but it was followed by a rush of anger. How could anyone think possessions were more important to them than serving and loving the King? What earthly thing could possibly be worth more than eternal treasure? The young man was certainly very foolish, Heart decided. There was nothing SHE wouldn't give up to obtain treasure in Eternal Palace!

She stayed a few minutes longer, gazing thoughtfully at the glorious Palace and thinking about King Vine and his Father, but her thoughts continually strayed back to the young man who loved his possessions more than he loved King Vine.

Finally, she got up and walked slowly down the mountain path, still wondering what it was that made the young man so unwilling to accept Word's message to him.

Heart stopped at the Stream of Refreshing and sat down to dangle her feet in its cooling water. Leaning back on her hands, she yielded herself to enjoy fully the soft breeze in her hair, the gentle sound of the rippling water, the caress of the soft carpet of grass beneath her. She closed her eyes and breathed deeply of the delightful scent of wild flowers. How happy and content she was!

Suddenly, her eyes flew open and she sat up straight ... listening.

Was it only the leaves rustling? No ... there it was again. It sounded like someone's muffled sobs. She looked around her in all directions, but there was no one in sight.

Heart jumped to her feet and began to walk toward the sound. The further she walked the more unmistakable the sounds were. She was sure, now, someone WAS weeping as though her world had come to an end. Cresting a knoll, Heart realized that she was only a short distance from Egypt. She stopped. Not even someone sobbing could trick her into entering Egypt. She had just made up her mind to turn and run in the opposite direction when she realized that whoever was crying was not in Egypt after all but just outside the gate.

Heart took a closer look at the small huddled figure. It looked like ... yes ... she was sure. It was Molly Miserable.

"Molly," cried Heart in surprise, "what are you doing here and whatever is the matter?"

Molly jerked, startled at the sound of Heart's voice. No one had ever found her here before, outside of Egypt. Gazing through her tears, she stared at Heart, and turned the question around. "What are YOU doing here?"

"I heard you crying," answered Heart gently. "Tell me, what is wrong?"

"WRONG!" Molly choked on her sobs. "Wrong? Tell me, what is RIGHT? EVERYTHING is wrong!"

Heart sat down beside Molly. "Can you talk about it?" she encouraged.

The kindness in her voice made Molly stop crying. She stared at Heart. No one ever spoke kindly to her. Why would this girl be so different?

"Why should you care?" she asked suspiciously.

"I care because King Vine cares," answered Heart.

"King Vine? Who is he that he should care?" Molly asked with scepticism.

"King Vine is Lord over Eternal City. He lives with his Father in Eternal Palace. His presence is everywhere, and Word is his messenger sent to tell the good news and invite everyone to become a citizen of Eternal City."

Molly forgot her tears. No one had ever spoken words such as these to her before. And never had she met anyone as kind as Heart. She sat staring, her thoughts tumbling over each other.

"How did you come to know King Vine?" she finally asked, as much to keep Heart from walking away as to have an answer to her question.

"I had to come to the cross and follow Humble along the Way of Forgiveness into Eternal City," explained Heart.

"I've never lived anywhere but in Egypt," mused Molly. "I would be afraid to leave."

"Afraid?" asked Heart in astonishment. "But why? You are not happy here, are you?"

Heart Longing and the Treasure Keys

"Happy?" Molly's laugh was hollow. "What is THAT? I am always miserable!"

A thought occurred to Heart, and she asked, "Is Mr. Destroyer your father?"

"No," answered Molly Miserable. "If he was, maybe then he would love me. No, it was bad enough when my father Morbid Miserable lived with us, but he left long ago, leaving me and mom with nothing. Mr. Destroyer is my uncle, and he offered my mother and me a home if we would work for him. We run his errands all day long. I never have time to do anything I like. My mother is miserable, too, and has no time for me. The only time I have to myself is the occasional time I run here to cry, where no one can hear me."

It was the longest speech Molly had ever made, simply because no one had ever wanted to listen to her that long. She looked searchingly at Heart wondering why SHE was listening. Could it be she really did care as she said?

Heart did not immediately reply to Molly. She found it hard to believe someone could live so miserable a life. What would it feel like to be in Molly's shoes? She thought of her own contented home and of King Vine who had made her life so happy and exciting. How could she help Molly? What could she possibly do for her?

Molly was looking at the gold cross and chain around Heart's neck. "Your necklace is very beautiful," she said.

"Oh yes," Heart agreed, reaching up to touch it. "It was my grandmother's. She wanted me to have it because I was her oldest granddaughter. It was her last gift to me before she went to live in Eternal Palace."

"I never had anything from someone who loved me. If I had a necklace from someone who loved me, maybe then I wouldn't be so miserable," said Molly.

A disturbing thought flashed through Heart's mind, but she quickly pushed it aside.

Molly got to her feet. "I have to go back. My mother will already be furious with me. Mr. Destroyer blames her if I'm not there to do my work."

Heart felt a burden of sorrow on her shoulders as she watched Molly slowly walk back into Egypt. With her head hanging down, she looked as dejected as anyone Heart had ever seen. *Poor Molly*, she thought with compassion.

Heart started on her way home, but her troubled thoughts kept her eyes focused on her feet. If only there was something she could do for poor, unhappy Molly. She had not gone far when she heard a familiar flapping of wings and looking up saw Conscience land on a branch above her. His sharp eyes were intently focused on her face.

"Give to the poor and you shall have treasure," he said clearly.

"But I don't have anything to give her, "she argued, hoping Conscience would fly away. She kept on walking, quickening her pace.

Conscience flew out of sight, to Heart's relief, and she hoped that he was gone for good. She turned off the path, not noticing a small sign that read "To Selfish Park". She had not followed the path for long when she came to a pretty little grassy area and sat down on the cool green carpet. Her thoughts were still on Conscience's words, and they upset her. What did he think that she had to give to Molly?

"You have your necklace." Conscience's sharp voice startled Heart. She turned to see him sitting on the grass not far from her. He made her feel most uncomfortable and she frowned at him.

She didn't want to hear what he was saying. How dare he? Her necklace was her most prized possession. It was all she had from her beloved grandmother. It was certainly unkind of Conscience to suggest she give it away. Maybe there was something else that she could give to Molly Miserable. One of her other necklaces, perhaps; she had several she never wore.

Heart was too aggravated to sit still, so she left the park area and continued down the path, keeping her eyes on the ground in case Conscience was sitting somewhere waiting to fasten his beady eyes on her again. Then, she heard the unmistakable flapping of his wings. He was still close by, but he did not say anything more. Though Heart dreaded to hear his voice, the fact that he didn't speak, somehow, bothered her even more. Finally, she shouted at him.

"Why my best necklace?" she demanded.

"To show Molly you really do care about her," answered Conscience quietly, yet the sharpness of his voice cut deep.

"But I could prove that to her by giving her one of my other necklaces. I'll even give her TWO of them!" suggested Heart, feeling generous.

"Only giving the best things gains treasure," answered Conscience firmly.

Heart's emotions battled inside her. She DID want to show Molly how much she cared and she DID so want treasure in Eternal Palace, but why did it have to cost her best necklace?"

Then, even as she asked, she remembered how she had judged that young man on Promise Mountain. Foolish, she had called him, because he didn't want to part with his possessions to gain Eternal treasure. Was she not just as foolish as he was?

Later that evening, Heart was helping her mother do the dishes.

"Something seems to be troubling you, Heart," observed her mother.

"I'm trying to decide something," answered Heart vaguely, then, on second thought, decided to confide in her mother. She told her about Molly.

"Oh, the poor child!" cried Mrs. Longing, overcome with compassion.

"Mother," asked Heart hesitantly. "Do you think it would be all right to give my cross necklace to Molly to show her that I love and care about her?"

"Why, Heart!" exclaimed her mother in surprise. "That would be a real sacrifice for you. That is your most prized piece of jewelry - your last gift from your grandmother. Are you sure you could part with it?"

Heart ignored her mother's question, and instead asked, "Do you think grandmother would mind?"

Heart Longing and the Treasure Keys

"I believe your grandmother would understand," answered Mrs. Longing-Fulfilled gently. "She was very wise about finding treasure." Mrs. Longing-Fulfilled quickly dried her hands on her apron and gave Heart a tight hug. "I'm sure she would be very proud of you, dear."

Heart's mind was suddenly made up, and she began to plan how she would find Molly. She couldn't, or rather she wouldn't, go into Egypt to find her, and she didn't know when Molly would come to the gate again. She wondered if Molly made a habit of going to the gate at the same time each day. Heart decided to go the next afternoon and, perhaps, Molly would be there. If not, she would have to think of some other way to meet her. She breathed a request to King Vine that he would guide her.

The next day, when Heart reached the gate to Egypt, no one else was there. She stood for some time looking over the gate, but she could not see a single person. The sounds of Egypt reached out to her, calling for her to come in, but they held no power of attraction for her.

She was about to turn away, thinking it was of no use to wait for Molly, when she heard the sound of young voices. Soon there came into view several boys running toward the gate, chasing a ball that was swiftly rolling away from them.

The ball rolled under the gate, and Heart grasped it. A lad came up to get it and held out his hand, shouting, "That's my ball!"

Heart held the ball behind her back and made no move to return it to the boy. "So, do you know Molly Miserable?" she asked.

"Yah, sure, everyone knows Molly," answered the boy rudely. "Come on, give me my ball."

"I will," promised Heart, "if you promise to take a message to Molly that someone is waiting for her at the gate."

"And what makes you think I would do that?" demanded the boy – then, seemed to have a change of mind. "Yah, okay... I'm going by there anyway, and maybe Mr. Destroyer will give me some candy. He does that sometimes. Maybe if I see her, I'll tell her."

Seeing it was the best she was going to get, Heart said ... "Thanks!" And tossed the ball back to him.

He ran off with his friends laughing. Heart really wasn't at all sure that her message would be delivered, but she sat down to wait just in case it would be.

Every few minutes, she got up to go look over the gate to see if she could see Molly coming. Even if the boy did give her the message, perhaps Molly would not be able to get away.

Heart was thinking about giving up and trying again another day, when Molly came running to the gate, breathless and red faced. She looked over the gate, searching.

"It's me, Molly, over here!" called Heart.

"Oh," said Molly, "what do you want? I'm already in trouble, and I'll be in more if I don't hurry back."

"I just wanted to tell you that I love you, and I want you to have this." Heart spoke quickly before she could change her mind. She took off her necklace, and reaching over the gate, fastened it around Molly's neck.

Molly stared, speechless, but her eyes spoke volumes. They filled with tears. "You want ME to have your best necklace? But it was your grandmother's. No one gives away their best!" she protested in disbelief.

"When they know the love of the King they do," answered Heart. "And I love you enough to give you my best!"

"It is the most beautiful thing that has ever happened to me," said Molly, her voice choked with a sob. "I won't mind if I get into trouble anymore. I'll just look at my necklace and know that someone loves me. You are the only friend I have!"

Watching Molly, Heart felt joy bubbling up within her, and to her surprise there was no pain in giving up her necklace. But she knew it wasn't enough. "Molly," she said, "King Vine wants you to come live in Eternal City too. Then you will never have to be miserable anymore. Won't you come, Molly?" she pleaded earnestly. "Please come. I'll go with you to the cross."

"Oh, I want to ... I really do!" said Molly, longingly, "but I couldn't leave my mother. I'm all she has."

"She can come too," urged Heart.

"I don't know, "Molly hesitated. "I just don't know. You know us, Heart. We wouldn't belong in Eternal City. And even if we did, Mr. Destroyer would never let us go."

Hearing someone scream her name, Molly turned, terror filling her eyes. "I have to go, Heart," she said quickly, "but thanks ... thanks a lot. I'll always remember you are my friend."

Then she was gone.

Heart Longing had dreaded giving away her necklace, knowing how much she would miss it. Yet, to her surprise, she did not miss it at all. In fact, it seemed more hers, now, than when it had still hung around her neck. Thinking about how happy it made Molly made her glad too. She was so thankful that she had not given in to foolishly keeping the necklace for herself.

That evening she unfolded her treasure map, and as she did, a key fell out. Even before she examined it closely, she knew it was the key to "GIVING WHAT YOU HAVE' treasure".

Heart added the key to her others. It was so much fun finding treasure. She wondered how it could possibly be even more joyous to receive the treasure, when she arrived in Eternal Palace.

CHAPTER 11

"A Visit to World City"

It was finally the day that the Longing-Fulfilled family had planned for some time. They were going to World City to visit Heart's aunt, uncle, and cousins – the Hard-Hearted family.

It was Heart's first thought as she bounced out of bed in the morning. She had not seen the Hard-Hearted family for a long time, not since she had left World City to live in Eternal City. She wondered what her cousins were like now. Had they changed? Would they think SHE had changed? Would they know it was because of King Vine that she was different?

The Longing-Fulfilled family were finally on their way. As soon as everyone was settled in for the journey, Heart took the opportunity to ask her father a question that had been puzzling her.

"Dad," she said, "I've been thinking about the time I went beyond the Eternal City wall into World City. It was wrong to go beyond the wall where the love of King Vine could not reach me, and I got myself into such trouble. How come we're all going to World City now? Aren't we heading into danger?"

"That's a good question, Heart," answered Mr. Longing-Fulfilled. "There is a big difference between the reason you had for going into World City and our mission today."

"What is the difference?" asked Trouble-Free. He, too, was interested to hear his father's explanation.

"Well, you see," his father began, "when you went beyond Eternal City's wall, Heart, you went in disobedience. You knew it was wrong to go, but you went anyway. When we walk in disobedience, we always move out of the blessings of Eternal City. But when we go to World City because the King sends us, and we go in obedience to tell others of his love, his Presence goes with us, and we do not cross the wall at all."

Both Heart and Trouble-Free were silent for a moment, considering their father's words.

"That's neat," Heart finally said thoughtfully. "We are going today, because the King sent us?"

"Yes," answered Mrs. Longing-Fulfilled, joining in the conversation. "The Hard-Hearted family, your aunt and uncle, as well as your cousins Connie Conceit and Noel Knowledge

Heart Longing and the Treasure Keys

do not know the King, and we are going to show them how wonderful living in Eternal City is."

"But will they listen?" questioned Trouble-Free, remembering how his cousin Noel loved to show off as a know-it-all.

"We don't know," said his father. "Our part is to go and tell them the good news and to show them that we truly are representatives of the King in all we say and do."

Heart was quiet for a long time, thinking about how she could show her cousins how King Vine had changed her. She had never before enjoyed visiting the Hard-Hearted home. Her cousins were loud and quarrelsome ... But ... maybe this time it would be different. SHE was different, and she was going because King Vine had sent her to go in his name.

"Oh, look!" exclaimed her mother, suddenly, pointing to a beautiful river winding far below the embankment on the left side of the road.

Mr. Longing-Fulfilled stopped the car, and everyone climbed out to stretch and enjoy the breathtaking view.

Heart wandered off to one side, still wondering how she could show her cousins the love of the King.

Hearing footsteps behind her, Heart glanced over her shoulder, expecting to see her father, but it was Word. Heart looked past him to see that he had tethered his horse on a nearby tree.

"Word," she smiled in greeting, wondering how he could have known she needed to ask him something. She looked up into his shining face and asked, "Word, how shall I show my cousins that I am different?"

Word returned her smile before he answered. "By your attitude, Heart. Show them that you have become like King Vine. Show them that gentleness is stronger than strife. Show them that a quiet answer turns away wrath. Show them that good is stronger than evil. Wear a meek and quiet spirit, which in the eyes of the King is a beautiful ornament. If you do this, you will find much treasure."

For the rest of the trip, Heart considered Word's message carefully so she would not forget it.

Arriving at the Hard-Hearted home, the Longing-Fulfilled family were given a surprisingly warm welcome. Even Connie Conceit and Noel Knowledge seemed pleased to see them. They were eager to show them the new pool and water slide in their backyard, and it wasn't long before Trouble-Free and Heart were having fun, even enjoying their cousins' company.

When they were finally exhausted, they lay down on the grass to dry off in the sun.

Connie then asked the question Heart knew she had been dying to ask since they had arrived. "How come you left to go live in Eternal City?"

Heart took a deep breath, asking King Vine to guide her words. She eagerly told of how beautiful it was in Eternal City and that nothing in World City could compare with the joy of knowing King Vine. She told how good and kind and loving he was and how much she looked forward to going to live with him in Eternal City.

When she finally stopped, her cheeks were flushed with the excitement of sharing the good news. She searched Connie's

Heart Longing and the Treasure Keys

face and was disappointed to see that she did not seem to be at all impressed.

"Posh," she scoffed. "I think it's much more fun in World City, and who wants to go to Eternal Palace? I don't want to go through that dark dismal door named "DEATH". Besides, just because you've met the King doesn't mean you have to go off and leave World City. I have a friend who's met the King, and she's just as much fun as she was before. She didn't change a bit, and she has no silly notions about leaving World City to live in Eternal City. If King Vine is so all kind and loving, why does he make his followers leave their family and friends?"

Heart did not know what to say. What could she say in answer to Connie's argument? Who could possibly WANT to stay in World City after they had met the King!

"Who are you talking about?" asked Noel Knowledge, who had kept one ear cocked in their direction so he could hear their conversation. "Is it Honey Sweet?"

Heart drew her breath sharply. Honey Sweet? Could it be the same Honey Sweet she knew? Her unspoken question was answered when Connie Conceit suddenly jumped to her feet and waving wildly yelled at someone crossing the street some distance from where they all sat.

"Hey, Honey Sweet! Come over and talk to my cousin!"

A few minutes later, Honey joined the group. It WAS the same Honey Sweet that Heart knew. Honey smiled, her eyes never leaving Heart's face.

"Oh, Heart," greeted Honey. "It's sooo delightful to see you again. I've missed you soooo!! WHEREVER have you been hiding? Well, never mind, it's just sooo wonderful to be together again."

"Come on," said Noel Knowledge to Trouble-Free with a groan. "Let's go! It's much too STICKY around here, if you know what I mean. Anyway, I want to show you the latest project that I'm working on in my science class and I want you to see the new gadget I got for my birthday."

"Honey Sweet," began Heart, when the boys were gone, "Connie tells me that you've been to meet the King. I've never seen you in Eternal City." She looked at Honey, somewhat accusingly.

"Oh, sure, I met the King when you did. I followed you and Sally and Lily to the cross and I saw the King. But why do you insist on living in Eternal City? It's much too boring a place for me. All those restrictions - and rules! Yuck! Give me World City any day! I'm definitely a good-times girl, the life of the party, you know? Besides, I'm much too loyal to turn my back on my friends just because I've met the King. After all, doesn't he teach that we're to love everyone?"

"Well, yes, of course," agreed Heart, "but how can you love them when you are living in World City where there is no real love?"

"How little you know," laughed Honey Sweet, with a condescending smirk. "You think all I do is care about me, right? Well, just let me tell you. I know all about treasure hunting, and I'm sure I have a great deal more in my possession than you do!"

She paused to enjoy Heart's look of confusion, then she continued. "There's this rich family that lives not far from

Heart Longing and the Treasure Keys

me. I take care of their children every afternoon. I've earned enough money from that alone to buy the most gorgeous horse you ever did see."

"You think earning money is gathering treasure?" asked Heart, hoping she had somehow misunderstood.

"Well, of course, dummy," snorted Honey, almost sounding like a horse. "What good is treasure if you can't enjoy it?"

"But the Eternal treasure is a forever treasure. King Vine keeps it safe until we come to live with him," explained Heart.

"I hate to wait for anything," whined Honey. "I want what I want NOW, and I want to enjoy it while I'm young. Besides, I'm sure when I DO go to Eternal Palace I'll have just as much treasure as you!"

"I think you are both going to be surprised when we get to Eternal Palace and you see how much treasure I'll have," interrupted Connie, resenting that she was left out of the conversation. "I live as good as I can. There's nothing I don't do well, and if there really are treasure chests in Eternal Palace, I'm sure mine will be the biggest of them all." Connie Conceit's voice was full of self-pride as she spoke with her nose in the air.

Heart was listening quietly to Honey and Connie trying to outdo each other. She knew they were not followers of King Vine, but how could she tell them that they were not gathering any treasure at all?

Finally, Honey Sweet turned to Heart.

"Well, we haven't heard much from you. You haven't told us how YOU gather treasure. How much do you have?"

Heart wanted to tell them about the things she had done for King Vine and how she had been held prisoner in Egypt and how she had helped rescue two boys from falling down a cliff. But just when she opened her mouth she remembered Word's advice about a meek and quiet spirit, and somehow she knew that bragging was not what pleased King Vine. So all she said was, "I don't know how much treasure I have. I try to be obedient to Word's messages and live so that King Vine will be pleased. He decides how much treasure I have found."

"Sounds pretty dumb to me," said Connie with a shudder. "Come on girls, let's go to the playground just around the corner. They've set up some new exciting rides."

The three girls raced each other to the playground. Connie led the way to her favourite ride – an oversized slide that twisted and turned with a dark tunnel through the center and then opened up into a large pool of water. Some younger children were waiting for their turn to enjoy the long slide. Connie roughly pushed them aside.

"Go play somewhere else," she ordered.

One of the little girls began to cry. "But I have been waiting for a long time – it was my turn."

Heart went to put her arm around the child, and said comfortingly, "Come, you can ride with me. We'll go together, okay?"

Connie scowled at Heart, but Heart did not notice.

When they had tired of the rides, they found they were thirsty, and Honey Sweet suggested they go get raspberry snow cones at the playground snack bar.

Heart Longing and the Treasure Keys

Heart was glad she still had some change in her pocket from the money her father had given her yesterday. It was just enough to pay for a regular sized snow cone.

They were just walking away from the snack bar when a young boy, jostled playfully by his friend, bumped into Connie Conceit. Her cone flew out of her hand and landed in the dust.

"You stupid idiot!" exploded Connie. "Just look what you've done. You buy me another cone!" she ordered angrily.

The little boy stared with big frightened eyes at Connie. His lip began to tremble as he said, "But I have no money!"

"Never mind, Connie," said Heart soothingly. "Here you can have my cone. I'm not very thirsty after all."

Connie looked at Heart with a strange expression but said nothing, taking the offered cone.

Later, as the two families were enjoying the evening meal together, Connie told how she had lost her snow cone because of a rude little boy.

"You poor thing!" pitied her mother. "What did you do? I hope you made him pay!"

"I tried," said Connie tearfully, "but he had no money, and I had none left. I had to go without. I was sooo thirsty!"

Heart watched, shaking her head and wondering how Connie could make her eyes fill with tears at will like that. She certainly did sound convincing.

"Well, you just never mind," consoled her father, reaching into his pocket for a handful of change. "Here, here's enough to buy yourself two cones tomorrow, seeing you had to go without today!"

Connie took the money, her tears gone. She glanced sideways at Heart, almost daring her to give her away, but Heart said nothing. As Connie looked into Heart's steady gaze something unfamiliar stirred within her. She had never felt guilty before.

After they had left the table, Connie said to Heart, "I suppose you expect me to share the money with you because you didn't tell on me. Well forget it; I'm not sharing."

"No, I don't want any of your money," said Heart quietly.

"You don't?" Connie stared at Heart. "Boy, you sure are different than you used to be. I've never known anyone like you before."

On the way home, Heart dozed in the back seat, half-listening to her parents talk about the day's visit. Heart wondered if Connie would think about what she had told her about King Vine.

Hearing a familiar rustle, Heart opened her eyes to see Word riding alongside the car. She waved at him through the open window.

Word trotted his horse closer to the window and held out a treasure key to Heart. "It is the key for the treasure for those who have a 'MEEK AND QUIET SPIRIT'," praised Word. "You have made King Vine proud of you today. You have gathered much treasure."

Heart held the key tightly in her hand all the way home, thinking about Connie and Honey and asking the King to show them how much he wanted them to come live with him in Eternal City.

CHAPTER 12

"A Secret Bouquet"

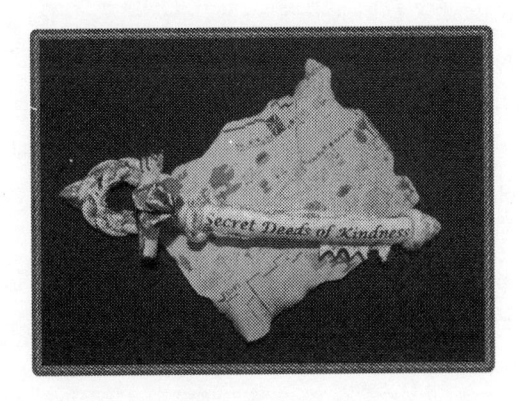

It was breakfast time in the Longing-Fulfilled home, and the family was enjoying bacon and eggs with fluffy biscuits around the table. It was a rare morning when no one needed to rush off somewhere.

"My sympathy really went out to her," Mrs. Longing-Fulfilled was saying. "It's been years since her husband died and still she talks about him as though he just stepped out the door for a few minutes."

"Who is this, Mom?" asked Heart, curious to know who her Mom was talking about.

"It's the little old widow who's just moved into the house on the next street over from us. It seems she has no family and can't get out much so she has not yet made any friends here. She's very lonely. I'm going to make a point of visiting her regularly," resolved Mrs. Longing-Fulfilled.

"Good idea," agreed Mr. Longing-Fulfilled. "Why don't you invite her over for supper some evening soon?"

"I will! We'll do it this week," promised Heart's mom enthusiastically.

"What's she like, Mom?" asked Trouble-Free.

"She's very nice. You'll all like her." Mrs. Longing-Fulfilled smiled at Miss Favor. "She's like the grandma in the last story I read you."

"How sad not to have any family," said Heart Longing, thoughtfully. "She must have loved her husband very much to still miss him so deeply."

"Yes," answered Mrs. Longing-Fulfilled. "She was telling me that today would have been their sixtieth wedding anniversary. Her husband was a quiet man, not given to many words, but on every anniversary he would leave a bouquet of flowers somewhere for her to find. It was his way of saying, 'Happy Anniversary'. She still misses those yearly bouquets."

A tiny thought sprouted in Heart's mind and it began to grow. She stared into her cereal bowl, a smile playing at the corners of the mouth. Her family's voices blurred, her own thoughts shutting them out … until her father's words brought her back to the present. "I talked to Word last night, and he said something very interesting. I haven't been able to forget it."

Heart leaned forward eagerly. She was always interested in what Word said.

Her father continued. "Word said, 'Take care, don't do your good deeds publicly to be admired, for then you will lose your reward. When you do a kindness to someone, do it secretly, and the King who knows all secrets will reward you openly.'"

Heart felt her pulse quicken. That message was for her! She just knew it was, but how could Word have known what she was planning?

When breakfast dishes were cleared away and the kitchen once more in tidy order, Heart hurried outside, running all the way to her favourite flowering meadow. There she picked the most beautiful blooms until she could carry no more.

Stopping at the Fort of Refuge, she arranged them carefully in a glass vase she'd left there several days before. Looking at her rainbow-hued bouquet critically from all sides, she smiled in approval. It was perfect!

She began to walk in the direction of the widow's house. She walked slowly, so as not to disturb the delicate flower petals or jostle the water out of the vase. She walked even slower as she neared the widow's home. What if she were outside? What if she saw her? How would she explain the flowers? As she drew nearer, she saw, to her relief, that the yard was empty and the window blinds were still drawn shut.

Heart stole quietly into the yard and hardly daring to breathe, crept up the steps onto the veranda. There, on a little table, she placed her bouquet of flowers. She was almost back down the stairs when the last one creaked sharply. She froze and heard the quick tapping of a cane. Someone was coming!!!

Oh, no! What if she's seen me? thought Heart in a panic. Quickly, she darted behind a thick shrub and crouched down. She was well hidden from view of anyone on the veranda but peering through the shrub's branches, she could still see the table with the flowers.

The door opened, and an elderly lady slowly stepped outside. Her hair was white, her face soft and gentle looking. She was wearing a blue dress that Heart saw matched her eyes when she looked around her yard to see what had caused the sound. She did not immediately notice the table holding the flowers as she stood in the open doorway, but then Heart heard her exclamation of delight!

"OH, how lovely! How beautiful!" she murmured. "A messenger of the King must have brought them to remind me I am still loved. Oh, how blessed I am."

Carefully, the little widow lady carried the flowers into the house in one arm and used her cane with the other. Heart stole away unnoticed.

She smiled, remembering the widow's words – "a messenger of the King" – Well, she really was, wasn't she?

She was still warm with the glow of her secret, when rounding a curve in the path, she almost bumped into Honey Sweet.

Heart Longing and the Treasure Keys

"Hey! Watch where you are going!" scolded Honey, her usual sticky-sweet smile hiding behind a dark scowl. "You almost ruined my cake!"

Honey Sweet was carrying a huge cake, beautifully decorated with entwining red roses at the foot of a lovely cross. It was the most beautiful cake Heart had ever seen. "Who is it for?" she wondered.

"Haven't you heard?" asked Honey Sweet dramatically. "King Vine is going to be on Promise Mountain today. People are going to bring him gifts. I'm going to give him this cake. I KNOW it will be the most beautiful gift, and I know I shall receive the biggest reward."

"I'm sure he will love it," agreed Heart. She couldn't help feeling keenly disappointed that she had not known the King was coming. Now she had nothing to give him.

"Why don't we go together?" Honey Sweet asked generously. "You ARE going to the Mountain, aren't you? I can't believe you didn't know the King was coming. I mean, with you being such a great friend of his and all." Her voice dripped with sarcasm.

Heart ignored Honey's barbs and answered quietly. "Yes, I'm going to the Mountain." She wouldn't miss a chance to see King Vine for anything, but how she hated to go empty handed. She looked almost enviously at Honey Sweet's lovely cake. They passed several people along the way, all of whom exclaimed in admiration of Honey's cake.

"The King will surely reward you greatly for giving him such a gift!" they praised, and Honey smiled back proudly.

Honey looked pointedly at Heart's empty hands.

"Too bad you don't have something to bring the King," she commented unkindly.

Honey Sweet's words stung, but Heart answered with a gentle smile. "If I can just see him, I will be happy. Besides I will be glad just to see you receive your reward."

Honey's eyes gleamed with anticipation. "What do you think my reward will be?"

"I don't know," answered Heart honestly.

"What is THAT?" exclaimed Honey suddenly, plainly disgusted. She nodded her chin toward something just up ahead to the left of the path.

Heart stopped, and looked in the direction of Honey's disdainful gaze. "Why," she gasped, "it's a boy crying!"

She ran ahead and knelt beside the weeping boy.

"Whatever is the matter?" she asked.

"I did so want to go and see the King. I started off with my brothers. They promised to help me, but I couldn't keep up because of my lame foot, and they've run off ahead without me."

"Come ON, Heart!" urged Honey insistently. "We can't waste time on a snivelling, crippled boy. Never mind him! We'll be late seeing the King if we don't hurry."

Reading Heart's intentions, she added quickly, "And NO, you cannot carry him, Heart! He's too heavy and I won't help. I've got my cake to carry. Now, are you coming or not?" Honey scowled, tapping one foot.

Heart looked up at Honey. "Go ahead, Honey," she said. "We'll follow as quickly as we can."

Heart Longing and the Treasure Keys

When Honey saw that Heart had made up her mind to help the boy, she made another disgusted sound and walked on without another word.

The boy looked at Heart gratefully, his tears forgotten.

"Can you walk on your lame foot at all? Can you walk if you lean on my shoulder?" asked Heart kindly.

"Yes, I think so," he said eagerly, hope rising within him. "But why did you stop to help me? Everyone else just passed by."

"You want to see the King, don't you?" asked Heart, ignoring his question. "Well, I'm here to help you. Come, let's go!"

With the boy leaning heavily on Heart's shoulder, the going was very slow. Neither of the two spoke; it took all of their concentrated effort to move as quickly as possible. Both were thinking eager thoughts of seeing the King. They were forced to rest frequently. Many travellers passed them by, but none offered their help. Heart hoped they would not be too late to see the King.

Finally, the Mountain was in sight. A huge crowd blocked their view, and Heart's hopes sank within her. She couldn't see if King Vine was there or not.

"Is he there?" asked the boy eagerly. "When shall we see him?"

"I don't know. I can't see through the crowd," answered Heart, swallowing a lump of disappointment.

The two stood at the edge of the crowd, not daring to press in, for fear of being knocked to the ground.

Then, quite suddenly, without any explanation, the crowd parted, leaving an open pathway between them and the King!

"There, do you see? There, there is the King!" Heart pointed to the King, looking down at the boy to see if he could see him.

The boy was staring at the King, his eyes wide with wonder. "Yes, I see him. He is beautiful, and he is looking at ME! Why, why ... he LOVES me." Tears of joy filled the lad's eyes and spilled over his cheeks. Suddenly, it was all worth it! How glad she was that she had stopped to help the boy.

Then the crowd closed in again, blocking the King from view, but it did not matter. They had seen him!

"Hey, you made it after all!" boyish voices shouted, and Heart turned to see two boys who were obviously the brothers who had run off, leaving their lame brother to fend for himself. "Well, we needn't hurry on the way home. Come on, let's go."

Grasping their brother's arms, they began to help him down the path. He turned once and spoke his thanks to Heart with his eyes. Heart smiled to say she understood, then turned back to search the crowd. She wondered if Honey had given her cake to the King.

She could not find Honey in the crowd of people and finally turned to follow the path homeward, feeling alone and disappointed because she had had nothing to give the King. He had not even seen her. However, she was comforted by the memory of seeing the joy in the boy's eyes when he had seen the King looking at him. Heart suddenly realized that she did not even know the boy's name, or where he was from. Would she ever see him again, she wondered?

Heart Longing and the Treasure Keys

The next day, Heart was out looking for Word. Catching sight of several people gathered at the Stream of Refreshing, she walked over, hoping that she would find Word there.

"There she is! That's her! That's her!" an excited voice shouted as she approached. Suddenly, all attention was focused on her.

Heart stood still, puzzled and somewhat embarrassed, until the owner of the voice separated himself from the crowd.

Heart recognized the little lame boy she had helped the day before. But something was very different.

"Your foot!" cried Heart. "You are not limping anymore!"

"No," answered the boy with a joyous shout and a leap into the air. "Thank you for taking me to see the King. He healed my foot! He made me whole!"

Heart could not speak for the emotion that choked out her words. She felt waves of happiness for the boy, the wonder at the King who had healed him, and joy that she had had a part in bringing the boy to the King. It was an overwhelming flood of emotions.

Word stepped out from the crowd, and with a broad smile, walked over to Heart. He held something out to her. It was a new treasure key.

"Here is the key to the treasure rewarded to those who do secret deeds of kindness," he said in answer to Heart's puzzled look. "The King was pleased with the gifts you brought him," Word added warmly.

Heart looked up in surprise. "Oh, but there must be some mistake. I had nothing to bring him."

"The King saw the flowers you brought the widow lady, and he saw you bring the lame boy to him. Those are the gifts you brought to him," praised Word.

Heart reached out to take the key Word was still holding out to her. She smiled up at Word. "Thank you," she said simply, but her eyes were shining.

Heart was especially eager to show her father the new key for "SECRET DEEDS OF KINDNESS", and tell him what Word's message had meant to her. She decided to take a shortcut home. The shorter route took her past "SELFISH PARK". She would not have stopped, but as she was passing by she saw Honey Sweet, sulking on the bench.

"Honey Sweet!" she called. "Why are you so glum? Did you not receive a reward for your lovely cake?"

"Go away!" retorted Honey ungraciously. "I don't want to see YOU of all people. If you had helped ME instead of that silly lame boy, maybe the King could have had his cake, and I would have my reward."

"What do you mean?" asked Heart, sitting down on the bench beside Honey. "Whatever happened?"

"Oh," cried Honey as though the memory brought fresh pain. "I was SO close, I could have touched him. I reached out to give him my beautiful cake when someone bumped me, and the cake fell. The people weren't looking where they were going, and they trampled it into the ground. It was ruined!"

"Oh, I am sorry!" Heart said sincerely.

"Sure you are!" Anger crept into Honey's voice. "You'd think he could have at least acknowledged the gift. He saw it before it fell. I know he did. He just looked at me with the saddest look in his eyes and turned away."

Honey looked at the keys around Heart's neck. "I heard you managed to get a reward after all. I just don't get it!"

Heart thought of something Word had said, "If you do something to be admired you will lose your reward." Poor Honey Sweet! How could she help her?

Heart looked at the bench they were sitting on. "Did you see the name of this bench?" she asked.

"Leaning Bench?" answered Honey with a puzzled frown.

"Yes," answered Heart. "There are two ways of leaning. We either lean on ourselves and our own selfish ways, or we lean on King Vine and do the things Word tells us to do."

Honey looked at Heart thoughtfully.

"Could you explain to me why I lost my reward and you found yours?" she asked, a new humility in her voice.

"I would love to, Honey Sweet, and then we can search for treasure together," answered Heart warmly as the two girls walked off arm in arm.

CHAPTER 13

"Eternal Palace"

Heart's feet felt like they were wearing shoes of stone. It took all her strength just to lift one foot in front of the other, yet, her head felt as light as a feather, giving Heart the sensation that it could just float away. She was cold, so very cold. No, wait, she was hot. She was burning hot! Then she was cold again and glanced up at the sun to see why it had taken away its warmth. Why did it seem that home was such a long way off when she could see it just a short distance away? It seemed that with each step that she took towards it, it slipped a little further away.

Finally, she reached the door, and with her last bit of strength pushed it open.

"Mom." She tried to call, but the familiar word only vibrated in her head. Her tongue refused to form the sounds into intelligent words. Everything was floating, floating far away. She never noticed that she crumbled to the floor.

Mrs. Longing-Fulfilled thought she heard the front door open and then a 'thump'. She listened, then called, "Heart, is that you, dear?" But there was no answer.

Puzzled, Mrs. Longing-Fulfilled went to look and found Heart on the floor just inside the front door. Alarmed, she called Mr. Longing-Fulfilled, who came quickly and carried Heart in his strong arms to her bed.

"She's burning with fever," worried Mrs. Longing-Fulfilled, laying her hand on Heart's forehead. Heart stirred and tried to speak.

"Just rest, Heart," soothed her father. "You'll be alright. We'll send for the doctor. He'll be here soon."

The front door banged, and Trouble-Free shouted, "Anyone home?"

Mr. Longing-Fulfilled met Trouble-Free in the hall and asked him to be quiet because Heart was very ill. He sent him to go fetch Doctor Human Wisdom as fast as he could.

Never had Trouble-Free ridden his bike so fast, and it wasn't long at all before the doctor was at Heart's bedside.

He listened to her chest, looked in her ears and throat, took her temperature and then pulled a bottle out of his bag, handing it to Mrs. Longing-Fulfilled.

"I think it's just a case of the flu," he said. "She'll be alright in a few days. Plenty of rest, lots of fluids. I'm going on vacation, but I'll stop by when I get back. Don't worry!"

"Thank you, Dr. Wisdom," said a relieved Mrs. Longing-Fulfilled, glad to hear it was nothing serious.

But Heart was not any better over the next couple of days. The medicine did not seem to make any difference. Then, Heart took a turn for the worse. She just lay still without opening her eyes. She did not respond to any voices or movement around her. Mr. and Mrs. Longing-Fulfilled, Trouble-Free, and Miss Favor looked at one another, their worry furrowed on their brows. If only Dr. Wisdom hadn't gone away. There was no one else they could call.

Miss Favor began to cry. "Isn't Heart going to get better?" she sobbed.

Mrs. Longing-Fulfilled hugged her little daughter. "Yes, Miss Favor, Heart will get better, I'm sure." She tried to hide how anxious she really was.

"But the doctor isn't here to come help her," worried Miss Favor.

"No," answered Mr. Longing-Fulfilled, his voice shaking a little. Then it grew strong again. "No, the doctor isn't here, but we CAN trust King Vine. He is always ready to hear us and help us."

"Yes, yes!" cried Miss Favor, her face breaking out into a sunny smile. "The King - he will make Heart better again."

An idea formed in her little head, and catching Trouble-Free's attention, she motioned with her hand that he should follow her. They tip-toed quietly from Heart's bedroom.

Heart Longing and the Treasure Keys

Once outside, she turned eagerly to her brother. "You know how much Heart loves to sit on top of Promise Mountain? Well, why don't we get her friends, and we'll all go up Promise Mountain, and we'll ask King Vine to make her better!"

Trouble-Free stared at Miss Favor. "That's the best idea you've ever had! Now why didn't I think of that? Come on, let's find her friends."

Not long after, a small crowd could be seen climbing Promise Mountain.

Heart did not know anything except that her world had dissolved into pain and darkness. Every part of her ached and throbbed. The pain was like a heavy blanket, suffocating her, crushing her. She wanted to ask someone to move it away, but all that escaped her lips was a moan.

Mrs. Longing-Fulfilled held a cup of water to her mouth, but Heart could not drink it. Over and over in her mind she whispered, "King Vine, King Vine". If only she could go to him, surely he would make her well. But she couldn't go, she couldn't move. All her limbs had turned to stone, the weight of them was more than she could bear.

Then, very softly, she heard the beloved voice of the King. He was calling her name; he was calling her to come to him.

She tried to call back that she couldn't move. She was pinned down by the weight of the blanket over her. She tried to tell him, but the words did not come. She struggled to free an arm, a leg, but it was useless to try.

Then an amazing thing happened. Suddenly, the blanket was gone – the pain was gone – the heaviness in her body was gone. Heart felt light and free and full of strength and energy.

The King called again, and Heart hurried to find him. She knew where he would be. He would be waiting for her on Promise Mountain.

She was aware of a new strangely delightful sensation in her feet. It was like they were wings rather than feet – she could move them so effortlessly, and the speed at which she was moving was incredible.

In no time, she could see the top of the Mountain. She waved and called out to King Vine that she was coming. She was almost there!

Then suddenly she stopped, a sinking dread flooding through her mind. She had completely forgotten about the door. The "DEATH" door.

As she turned her eyes to where the door was in the high wall, she saw to her intense relief and joy that the door stood wide open, and the glorious light from Eternal Place was flooding through. With a glad cry she began to run toward the door. She ran so effortlessly – like she was weightless – what a joyful thing it was to run! She laughed in delight, knowing she could run forever and never know fatigue.

Just before she reached the door, she turned her head and saw the group of children kneeling on top of Promise Mountain. She recognized her friends and called eagerly to them. "Come with me! The door is open. We can go into Eternal Palace!" But they didn't seem to hear her and after Heart stared at them wonderingly for a moment, she decided she couldn't wait. With

Heart Longing and the Treasure Keys

a rush of joy, greater than she had ever known, she ran through the door to the other side.

And there – there was King Vine waiting for her, a glad welcoming smile on his shining face of love.

Heart threw herself into his arms. "King Vine, how I have longed to come!"

"And how I have waited for you!" responded the King, holding Heart close to his side.

Heart eagerly looked around her. How indescribably beautiful, how marvellously wonderful everything was. Glory upon glory stretched as far as she could see. If time was anything less than forever, Heart thought she could not begin to enjoy it all.

Before a shining white throne stood a crowd of worshippers blending their voices in such sweet harmony and glorious praise that Heart was drawn to them. How she longed to join them in their song. She looked to King Vine for permission.

He smiled. "There will be time, dear little Heart, but first I want to show you something."

He led Heart to a beautiful room. Heart gasped - unable to take in what she was seeing. It was the Palace treasure room and OH, what a treasure room it was! Totally indescribable. There stood chest upon chest, countless chests, pure shining gold chests filled with sparkling treasure.

She recognized some of the names on the chests and began to eagerly search for the names of her friends. Some of the chests were full of treasure, some were half full, and some had only the bottom covered. Some had only one treasure in them – the treasure of Eternal Life. Honey Sweet's chest was one of these. She looked for Connie Conceit's name, but could not find it.

Heart did not fully understand, but she knew that somehow the glories of Eternal Palace were hidden in the treasure one gathered in Eternal City. How sad it must be for someone to come to Eternal Palace and have to miss the wonders prepared for them because they had no treasure stored up for them. Heart's eyes filled with tears, and looking up, she saw the King's eyes were full of tears too.

"I want so much for my children, but some refuse to gather treasure and are in danger of losing what they do have." But then he smiled and said," Have you found your chest yet, dear Heart?"

No, she hadn't, and Heart began to search for the chest with her name on it. When she finally found it, she stood a moment admiring the lettering of her name on the side. The chest stood locked. Heart took the keys from around her neck and fitted every one into the locks. When she had turned the last key, she stepped back in stunned amazement. The chest lid swung open to reveal that not only was it full, it was overflowing with treasure! Shining gold, silver and jewels more beautiful than any she had ever seen lay in her chest.

"Heart." Heart turned at the sound of her name to look into King Vine's face.

"Come," he said. "I want to show you something more." He led her to another part of the room where empty treasure chests were stacked against a wall.

Heart Longing and the Treasure Keys

"What are these for?" asked Heart. "They look empty and have no names on them."

"These chests are waiting for people who have not yet come to the cross. They are for those who have not yet become citizens of Eternal City, who have never even begun to gather treasure."

"But what are those people waiting for?" asked Heart.

"Come, I will show you," answered King Vine and led her to a window. "Look," he said, pointing.

Heart looked and saw far below her – even though it was a great distance away, she could see as clearly as if it were very close. She knew what she was to look at, a man who was sitting outside a house.

She stared for a moment, and then exclaimed, "I know him! He is Mr. Regret. He says it is too late for him to leave Egypt."

"No, it isn't too late. I am still waiting for him. I love him," said the King softly.

"And there," pointed Heart," there is Molly Miserable. She is afraid to leave Egypt."

"She need not be afraid," replied the King. "I love her too. She would be safe if she would put her trust in me."

"And there," exclaimed Heart again. "There are Connie Conceit and Noel Knowledge and Jim Rough and Tim Tough and ... so many others!"

"Yes," answered King Vine. "I love all of them. I am waiting for them to come to the cross."

"But why don't they come?" asked Heart.

"They need someone to tell them I love them, and I am waiting for them, for I have prepared a place for them here. Do you know someone who could go tell them, dear Heart?"

Heart looked up into the King's lovely face. Did he mean for her to go back and tell them? She just COULDN'T leave now, not when she'd just come. She had only begun to see all the wonderful things in Eternal Palace. To go back would be so very hard!

Heart looked thoughtfully at the King, then turned to look back down at Mr. Regret and Molly Miserable, then turned again to gaze at the glory of Eternal Place.

"I want to stay here forever," said Heart slowly.

"You will be here forever," promised the King. "But if no one tells them ... they will never come."

"I really want them to come," said Heart. "If I go back, will it be long before I can return here?"

"No," promised the King lovingly. "It will not be long. As soon as your work is done, I will call you, and then you will come, bringing many with you. Then you will stay forever."

Heart sighed deeply, and then said, "Okay then. I will go back. I will tell them how much you love them and want them to find much treasure waiting for them when they come to Eternal Palace."

"You are a good servant, dear Heart." The King laid his hand on her shoulder, and together they walked back to the door named "DEATH". Heart walked through and heard it close gently behind her. She stood for a moment and looked at the door that had once seemed so fearful. Never again would

Heart Longing and the Treasure Keys

she be afraid of the door. She, now, knew what was on the other side.

Heart opened her eyes, and to her surprise found herself in her own bed. Her parents were kneeling beside her bed, crying. She reached over and touched them. "Please, don't cry," she begged. "I'm better. The King has sent me back with messages for the people he loves. Where are Trouble-Free and Miss Favor?"

Through tears - now tears of joy - Mrs. Longing-Fulfilled explained that they were up on Promise Mountain asking the King to heal her.

"I'll go tell them that he has already answered," laughed Heart, feeling her old self again.

Jumping out of bed, laughing at her parents' protest, she ran all the way to where her friends were still kneeling. Joyfully, she called to them and a cheer went up when they saw Heart standing strong and well before them. Heart pointed to Eternal Palace. It was so hard to believe but SHE had been there! "I was there," she told them excitedly. "And I saw the treasure chests!"

"You did?" "Did you see mine?" "And mine?" Everyone wanted to know.

Heart described what she had seen, and heard, and why she had come back.

"We must tell everyone how much the King loves them and show them by our actions who he is. We must gather treasure and help others to gather treasure so no one's chest will be empty when we go to Eternal Palace."

With awe and a new respect in their faces, the little group gathered around Heart. "What shall we do first?" they asked.

"First, I must go see Mr. Regret and Molly Miserable and tell them what the King said. Sally and Lily, will you come with me?" asked Heart.

With keen eagerness, the three friends went to bring Mr. Regret and Molly Miserable the messages from King Vine and to lead them to the cross and into Eternal City.

Mr. Regret and Molly were the first of many that Heart and her friends brought to the cross to find forgiveness and eternal life. Each time someone knelt at the cross to give themselves to King Vine, Heart looked up into the face of her King to see that the joy she felt bubbling up within her was shining from His eyes too.

And so the adventures of Heart Longing continued until the day she once again entered Eternal Palace.

This time, to live forever with her King!

Glossary

Word is the Bible – Matt.4:4, I Peter 1:25

- **King Vine** is Jesus – John 15:5
- **The King's Presence** is the Holy Spirit of God/Jesus who is with us always to help us and comfort us, even though we cannot see Him, John 14:16,26
- **Heart Longing** is that part of us that longs for Jesus, longs to know Him and to become like Him – Psalm 84:2
- **Humble** represents the attitude we must have toward God and others. James 4:10, Romans 12:16
- **Story characters** represent the things in our life that help or hinder us from becoming like Jesus. Colossians 3:1-12,
- **Egypt** represents the world, which is contrary to God's kingdom. Matthew 16:26, I John 2:15-17 (Hebrews 11:6 gives the analogy)
- **Treasure of Egypt** is the 'fool's gold' the world promises. The treasure that looks real but does not last - it turns to dust. See Matthew 6:19

- **World City** represents the world that is outside of God's rules for His Kingdom. Everyone who is not born again makes World City their home. I John 2:15,16, John 14:17
- **Eternal City** is the Kingdom of Heaven that everyone who believes in Jesus is 'born into' and made a citizen of. Colossians 1:13,14, Ephesians 2:19
- **Eternal Treasure** is the treasure/rewards God promises to those who walk in obedience to Him and do those things that please Him. Matthew 13:44, Matthew 6:20
- **Eternal Palace** represents where God lives, His heaven, and His throne room. Revelations 4:2
- **Underground Forest of Persecution** speaks of all the ways we 'suffer' as Christians, where the world does not always understand us or treat us kindly.
- John 16:33 – Jesus warned us that it would not always be easy for us to live in the world but He promised that we do not have to be anxious because He has overcome the world. See also II Timothy 3:12, I Peter 3:14

For You to Think About

Chapter 1

1. Does God want us to search for treasure? See Matt.6:20. Do we have a treasure map showing us where the treasure can be found?

    See Psalm 119:19 (LTB) **Open my eyes to see wonderful things in your Word, I am but a pilgrim here on earth; how I need a MAP and your commandments are my chart and guide.**

    - Who helps us read the MAP and shows us how to find the treasure? John 14:26 We have the Holy Spirit, the Helper who helps us to understand and remember the things Jesus said. Who represents the Holy Spirit in our story? (the Presence)
    - Look at Proverbs 8:21(NKJV) It talks about treasure for the one who seeks it. *"That I may cause those who love me to inherit wealth that I may fill their treasuries."* A wealth of treasure in heavenly treasure chests!
    - Look at Proverbs 8:21(NKJV) It talks about treasure for the one who seeks it. *"That I may cause*

> *those who love me to inherit wealth that I may fill their treasuries."* A wealth of treasure in heavenly treasure chests!

2. Why do you think Promise Mountain is so beautiful? What does it represent?

    II Corinthians. 1:29, I Peter 1:4 …. When someone says they will give you something, do you sometimes make them, "Promise!"? When God makes a 'promise', when He says He will do something, can we trust Him? What are some of the promises God makes? Some are found in Exodus 20:12, Psalm 34:7, Philippians 4:19, Psalm 32:8, Proverbs 3:5,6, Philippians 4:13

Chapter 2

1. Heart and her friends found the 'map' hard to understand … but as they studied it, they figured it out. We have the Holy Spirit to help us understand God's Word … and God wants everyone to understand Him. There is an exciting verse in Luke 10:21 that tells us that God did not write our treasure map (the Bible) for wise men, but for CHILDREN.

2. When Heart Longing looked at Word, her face reflected the light from Word's face. Does II Cor. 3:18 say that the more we 'look into Jesus' face' - thinking about Him and wanting to be like him, the more other people will think we look like Him?

3. What does Egypt represent in our story? The world. What is 'the treasure of Egypt'? Heb. 11:26 tells us that Moses had to make a choice – either the treasures of Egypt or the treasures of Jesus' Kingdom. Which did he choose? Why do you think he wanted to rather serve God than be a ruler in Egypt?

   What would be 'treasures of Egypt' in your life?

   What about the TV shows/video games your parents don't want you to watch or play? What do you do when your parents are not home?

   What about the candy bar that tempts you and there is no clerk in sight?

   What about when your friends want you to do something you know is wrong … like try to smoke a cigarette or take drugs or drink alcohol?

   What other things could tempt you to 'go to Egypt' rather than do the things that please God?

4. Does the bible tell us about a "Way Provided" when we get into trouble? What 'way' is provided in I John 1:9. Does God always have a Way Provided for us when we stumble and lose our way or fall into one of Satan's traps? See God's promise in I Corinthians 10:13

5. When we know what God wants us to do, when is the best time to obey? What did Mr. Regret do wrong? Why is it harder and harder to obey when you make excuses and put off doing what you know you are supposed to do? (see Heb. 3:15) What happens to a soft lump of clay when you leave it in the sun? Is that a

picture of what happens to our heart when we do not want to do what is right, or put it off?

6. How did the girls end up in Egypt? Where did they begin to go wrong? Are our thoughts like the rudder of a boat that directs where it goes? Where does the Bible say we should keep our thoughts? - see Philippians 4:8, What is our attitude supposed to be to one another – How did Heart and her friends not have the attitude about others that Romans 12:10 tell us to?

7. Who was Mr. Destroyer? (one of Satan's names is Destroyer, see I Cor. 10:10)

8. Who was Mr. Destroyer's enemy? - (King Vine) - Did Mr. Destroyer really want to give the girls treasure? What does Satan always want us to do? (John 8:44 tells us he is a liar and he wants everyone to believe his lies so that we will not believe God and obey Him)

Treasure Key - "ETERNAL LIFE" – John 3:16, John 10:28

Chapter 3

1. II Timothy 2:26 tells us that Satan sets traps to 'ensnare' us. One trap is to tempt us to tell a lie. Lily, in our story fell into this trap. What was Word's message about lying? See Proverbs 21:6, Proverbs 6:2. What are some other snares Satan lays for us? How did Lily get out of the trap? Is telling the truth always the escape

out of a 'lie trap'? How can we follow Heart's example, to avoid being taken captive by Satan? Psalm 199:11
2. What did Heart and Sally do to find their treasure? Luke 6:35 Is it hard to love your enemies and do good to someone who is mean to you? See Bible story in Luke 10:29-37
3. Maybe we don't have any real enemies who want to hurt us, but what about the people who don't seem to like us very much, who are always doing things to 'bug' us? Is it enough to love those who are nice to us? What does Matthew 5:46-48 tell us about who we are to love?

Treasure Key – "LOVE YOUR ENEMIES" – Luke 6:35
Treasure Key - "HIDING WORD'S MESSAGES" - Psalm 19:11, Psalm 119:11

Chapter 4

1. Why was Heart's name written into the King's Memory Book? Did you know God really does have a Memory Book? See Malachi 3:16
Do you think your name is written in His book? How often?
2. Can you think of any stories Jesus told about someone/ something being lost? See Luke 15:4-9 Have you ever lost something? How did you feel when you lost it and how did you feel when you found it? Have YOU ever

been lost? How did that feel? When you were found how did you feel? How did the person feel who found you? Who was Jesus really talking about when He told the story of the lost sheep? All of us were lost before Jesus found us. Isaiah 53:6. Jesus is the good Shepherd who came to find us and make us His own. Has Jesus found YOU? Do you belong to Him? How did you feel when you asked Jesus to make you His, and how do you think He felt when you came to Him? See Luke 15:10. See Proverbs 11:30, Daniel 12:3

3. Little Lamb and Miss Favor did not think they would get lost. They were just going to go a little way into the forest. Can you be 'distracted' from doing what is right by thinking you will just do something once, or you will just do it a little bit ? Does that sometimes 'trap' you into going further than you wanted to? For example, You didn't get your homework done, but you don't want to get into trouble, so you tell your teacher you dropped it on the way to school and the wind blew it away. You were only going to lie once…but if you lie once is it easier to lie the next time? In Matthew 16:6 Jesus warns against 'leaven'… Leaven is always symbolic of sin, and a little bit of leaven grows and grows.

Treasure Key - "LOVING THE KING" – Malachi 3:16

Treasure Key - "FINDING THE LOST" – Luke 15:4-7, Proverbs 11:30

Chapter 5

1. Are you aware of your conscience? What is it? It is a 'helper' that God has given us, a little voice in our mind that reminds us to do right and it makes us feel guilty (a STOP sign) when we do something we know is wrong. I Timothy 1:19
2. Why did Heart and Trouble-Free quarrel? Because they were not thinking of each other, only what each selfishly wanted. When did the quarrel end? When Trouble-Free listened to Conscience. Does Jesus want us to be the kind of person who does not make trouble but rather makes peace? See Matthew 5:9
3. Can you think of any Bible stories where someone made peace? One story is found in Gen. 13:2-17
4. How do we know what 'right doing' is? If we do the things Jesus tells us to do, we know we are doing what is right. Luke 6:46 There is a verse in I John 1:10 that says if we always act in love, we cannot do anything wrong. – What is the greatest commandment of God? In Matthew 22:37-40 Jesus said if we obeyed two commandments we would be obeying all His commandments. What are the two commandments? Also see Luke 6:31 –What does this verse tell us about how to know what is right to do?
5. Can you think of a time when you made peace when there was trouble or a quarrel? How did that make you feel?

Treasure Key – "DOING WHAT IS RIGHT" – Prov. 11:18, Luke 6:31

Chapter 6

1. Why did Tom Thief and his friends not like Heart? Because they hated King Vine and so they also hated everyone who loved Him. Who hates us? Satan … Why? Because Jesus loves us and protects us from Satan. Jesus is much stronger than Satan. See I John 4:4 (this verse reminds us of the story in II Kings 6:8-23)

2. Tom Thief, Darcy Deceit and Pride wanted to steal Heart's treasure. Who wants to steal our treasure? Satan – see John 10:10. How does he try to steal from us? See Colossians 2:8, and I Timothy 3:6 He tries to make us believe a lie or he tries to make us proud. Why is Satan afraid you will read your bible? King David knew the answer. It is found in Psalm 119:11.

3. Jude 21 tells us to always stay where the love of Jesus can reach us. How do we move away from Jesus' love? When we feel sorry for ourselves, when we are selfish, when we are mean, when we speak angry words, when we are unkind or unloving. What can we do when we know we have taken a step away from being in Jesus' love? I John 1:9 says that He will quickly forgive us and wash the spots off our robe. (Rev.7:14) .Jesus is

always watching over us, and He speaks to us through our conscience to come back close to Him as soon as we begin to do the things that are not pleasing to Him.

4. Why did Heart Longing gave in to the temptation to go where she knew she should not go.. Are you ever tempted to do things 'your way'? Did you know that Satan tempted Jesus to go His own way instead of what His Father had told Him? In the story in Luke 4:3-13 what three temptations did Satan use ? How did Jesus not give in to Satan's temptations and lies? By remembering God's Words. Is that good for us to do too?

5. It is very easy to become proud of the good things we are or be proud of the things we can do well. What does I Corinthians 4:7 tell us we should remember? Instead of feeling proud, what should we feel about the good things we are or have? We should be thankful to God who gave them to us to use to help others.

6. Why is Humble stronger than Pride? Pride is Satan's sin - I Timothy 3:6 see Prov. 29:23, and James 4:6 and God does not want His children to be like Satan. God resists/fights against the proud person but helps those who are humble James 4:6

Treasure Key – "THE MORNING STAR" - Revelation 2:26-28

Chapter 7

1. Do we have a Fort of Refuge? A place we can go where we can find quiet and safety? Yes, Jesus is our refuge. He is our 'high place' where we can escape to and be safe. We do not need to be afraid when we run into His arms.

    See Proverbs .18:10, Deuteronomy 33:27, Psalm 61:3

2. I Peter 4:12-16 talks about two kinds of suffering. One kind God sees and rewards us for it, but for the other kind we do not get any treasure or reward. Think of examples for both kinds of 'suffering'.

3. Acts 7:54-60 tells the story of a man who was the very first martyr. He loved Jesus so much he didn't care if people threatened to hurt and even kill him. The people stoned him to death, but what happened to Stephen? See verse 56 How do you think Stephen felt when he could see the sky open up to reveal heaven and Stephen could see Jesus standing there looking down on him? How did Stephen feel toward the people who killed him? see verse 60

4. What does Jesus say in Matthew 10:28, John 16:33 about why we should not be afraid of people who want to hurt us?

5. In the story that Humble told Heart, the prince thought the maiden was very beautiful and he loved her so much. Do you think Jesus feels that way about you? What does it say in Psalm 45:11

Chapter 8

1. What is the most frightening thing that has ever happened to you? Is it less frightening if you have someone stronger than you with you in a scary place? If we belong to Jesus, we are never alone because He has promised never to leave us. And He tells us we do not need to be afraid,…,ever! When Heart was so afraid and cold in her cell, King Vine sent his messenger to warm her. What has Jesus done for you to comfort you or help you in a scary situation? See Hebrews 13:5,6 and in John 14:23 Jesus says He will come live with us/in us.

2. We have many stories in the Bible where people were in frightening situations and in each one God was there to help and rescue them. Some of the stories are:
Joseph – Genesis 37:23-28
Miriam – Exodus 2:1-10
Shadrach, Meshach and Abednego – Daniel 3:8-30
Daniel – Daniel 6:18-24
Acts 16:25-34 (what did Paul and Silas do that the girls in the cage also did?)

3. What treasure does Jesus give those who are willing to suffer rather than deny Him? See Rev. 2:10 What will Jesus give us if we are faithful to the end?

Treasure Key – "CROWN OF LIFE" – Matthew 5:12, Rev 2:10

Chapter 9

1. Have you ever looked forward to something really exciting and then something happened to spoil your plans? How did that feel?
2. What was the lesson that Mother Robin taught Heart?
3. Why did King Vine praise Heart for telling Miss Favor about Him and helping her to know how to please Him? I Peter 2-4 is talking about people who help others to live the way God wants them to. While this passage is directed to leaders, anyone can help someone to know Jesus and to obey His commandments. When we do that Jesus notices and rewards us with the CROWN OF GLORY.
4. Read Colossians 3:23-24 What do you think the word 'whatsoever' means? Could it be doing your homework? Or helping your Mom by doing chores? or babysitting your little brother or sister? or letting your sister borrow your favorite necklace or letting your brother borrow your baseball glove? Or running an errand for your neighbour? Do you grumble sometimes if you are asked to do something you don't want to do? If Jesus knocked on your door, and you answered it and Jesus asked you to do that very thing for Him that you just grumbled about, would you do it? Would you tell Him to go ask someone else? In the Colossians passage it says that Jesus will reward us for the things we do, if we do them as though we are doing them for Him.

5. Challenge – for a day or for a week try to think about doing everything you do for Jesus, as though He Himself asked you to do it – whether you are at home, or in school, or in the playground. At the end of your day or week think back on what kind of week it was. Was it a good one? Were you happy? Did you make other people happy?

Treasure Key – "AS UNTO HIM" – Colossians 3:23,24
Treasure Key – "CROWN OF GLORY" - I Peter 5:2-4

Chapter 10

1. Read Luke 18:18-27 Why did the rich young man go away sad? Have you ever wanted something really badly and then found out that it cost more than you thought? Did that make you sad too?
2. Molly Miserable was not happy In Egypt. Why? Can anything really make us happy if we do not have Jesus? See Ecclesiastes 2:10,11 – Solomon had more riches than any man ever had. He had everything he could wish for but he said nothing gave him any lasting satisfaction or happiness.
3. Have you ever given away something you really loved? Was it hard to give it away? How did you feel after you gave it away?

4. What does the Bible say about giving to others? Luke 12:31-34, Luke 6:38, II Corinthians 9:7, Mark 12:41-44, Matthew 10:42, Acts 20:35
5. Jesus talks a lot about giving. Do you think that because God is so generous, He wants us to be generous too? Is giving only about money? Or can it be things like words and kind deeds, our smiles, our time? If we obey Mark 12:30,31 and love God and our neighbour do you think we would also be generous in any way we can help someone else?

Treasure Key – "GIVE WHAT YOU HAVE" - Luke 6:38

Chapter 11

1. Why was it okay for the Longing family to go back into World City? See John 17:14,15 What does Jesus explain here to His disciples? Did the Longing family do what Jesus commanded His disciples to do in Matthew 28:19?
2. Why did Honey Sweet not live in Eternal City? Did she love the world (love herself) more than she loved the King?
3. What does it mean to be meek? See I Peter 3:4, and Proverbs 22:4 How did Heart show meekness?
4. Why does having a 'meek and quiet spirit' please Jesus? Is being meek and quiet the opposite of being loud

and prideful, always wanting to get even? How did Heart show a 'meek and quiet spirit'? Why did Connie Conceit get angry with Heart? Who would you rather have as a friend? What kind of friend are you?

5. There is a story of a very meek man, Moses, in Numbers 12. Did Moses talk back when others said something mean about him? Did he defend himself? Was he glad when God punished his brother and sister for talking against Moses?

6. What does I Peter 3:4 call a meek/gentle and quiet spirit? Does that make us beautiful to God?

Treasure Key – "MEEK AND QUIET SPIRIT" – I Peter 3:4, Proverbs 22:4

Chapter 12

1. Read Matthew 6:4 Do you know someone who is always bragging about what they have done? Do you like to be with a person like that? Would that kind of person ever do something good in secret? Is it fun to do something nice for someone in secret?

2. Why do you think Honey Sweet's cake was not pleasing to King Vine? What are some things that people say they are giving to God, but God isn't pleased? Does our attitude have anything to do with it? In the Old Testament book of Malachi God speaks to the Israelites who are bringing the best sacrifices

and they hate bringing them and God asks them an interesting question. See Malachi 1:8

3. In the following verses, what reasons does God give for not being pleased with the things people give Him? Isaiah 29:13, I Samuel 15:22, Isaiah 58:7, II Corinthians 9:7

Treasure Key – "SECRET DEEDS OF KINDNESS" – Matthew 6:4

Chapter 13

1. Do you know some Bible stories where someone died and came to life again? See I Kings 17, John 11:1-46, Mark 5:22-43, Acts 9:36:42
2. Are you afraid of the door named 'Death'? Should we be afraid? Is it like going from one room to another when you know someone you love is on the other side of the adjoining door? See II Corinthians 5:8, Philippians 1:21 How do we know Jesus is waiting for us? See John 14:1-3
3. What do you think heaven will be like? What are some of the things we are told about heaven? Make a list using these scriptures. John 14:2, Revelation 19:8, Revelation 3:5, Revelation 21:4, Revelation 21:21, Revelation 21:18-20, Revelation 2:7, Revelation 4:11, Revelation 7:16, Revelation 22:5, Revelation 22:4 Revelation 19:9

Contact author at juliefrompearls@gmail.com

Printed in the United States
By Bookmasters